Two Dead on Crystal Creek

By M. Sue Alexander

Two Dead on Crystal Creek
FIRST EDITION 2020, USA
Copyright © 2020 by M. Sue Alexander
Revised 2021 by Suzander Publishing

Book Cover by Christine Roszak

View M. Sue's Website and Facebook Page

www.msuealexanderbooks.com

Series Titles by Author

Time of Jacob's Trouble
Book 1: The Four Horsemen
Book 2: Beast
Book 3: Witness
Book 4: The Word
Book 5: Judgment
Book 6: Deceiver

Resurrection Dawn 2014 Series
Book 1: Resurrection Dawn 2014
Book 2: The Christian Fugitive
Book 3: Rebels in Paradise
Book 4: Veil of Lies
Book 5: The Anointing
Book 6: Countdown to Justice
Book 7: All Rise
Book 8: Unlikely Suspect
Book 9: Lethal Snapshot
Book 10: Purgatory
Book 11: April Fool's Day
Book 12: Reign of Errors

Independent Titles
Adam's Bones
Encounters of the God-Kind
The Forum
The Minister's Haunting
Tomorrow's Promise
Out of Time: The Vanderbilt Incident

Foreword from the Author

Readers may wonder where an author gets an idea for a particular story. From my experience, it can come from a dream, or something someone said that catches my attention, or out of thin air. This particular story was formulated one evening as my husband and I played cards with another couple. The Canasta contest was usually us gals against the guys. When they beat us more than twice in a row on the same evening, we would look at one another and say: *Two Dead on* . . . you get the gist of our remark. But we were teasing.

After several years, writing this story with that title caught up with me. Not long ago, I began hearing conversation in my head while at the sink doing the dishes. Since the story was showing itself right in front of me, I decided I might as well sit down at the computer and write it. No outline, I let the characters live out the story, trying to keep up. I hope you enjoy *Two Dead on Crystal Creek.*

Reader Comments

Intrigue, mystery, murder, cliffhangers, and the one-liners! Can't get any better writing! Storyline keeps you coming back for more. --Joyce Keller; TN.

"A good read with twists and turns to keep your interest. The story involves mystery and deals with grief and aging. I highly recommend the book." –Sharon Haller; CT

"There is a right time
for everything," Ecclesiastes 3: 1.

A Time to Die

1

Thursday, October 28th

THERE'S A LOT OF FATTY cells pumping up my stomach. I can feel them stretching my polyester pants. Bought them from Walmart on a whim. Didn't need them, but I love the color. Purple looks good with white hair. Today it's naturally frizzy because of the humidity.

I don't want to think about Monday, the worst day of my life.

Hell's bells, I want the fat to go away but it clings to me like my pants. I want to look like I did when I was twenty-two. That was before I married Arthur, when I dieted and lost fifteen pounds.

I was a good lookin' chick back then. Black hair, eyes as blue as a robin's egg. Five six, one-hundred twenty pounds. No pregnancies to weaken my stomach muscles back then. I'm Snow White now, the only thing I lack is the Seven Dwarfs trailing after me.

I tug at my white kinky curls, which I absolutely despise almost as much as my fat body. And those wrinkles? My goodness, Old Age drives truck tires over my face. Every day I see new ruts. My hands think they have to match my face. You'd think they were in a race to see who could look the worst. I wonder if I need to get a facelift.

"Mrs. Powell?"

I look up and realize I've been thinking too hard. Detective Lloyd Peters Jr. looks at me like I've lost my cotton-pickin' mind.

Well, maybe I have. What am I doing sitting in his office when I have a dozen other things that need to be done?

"What is it?"

"We were discussing Arthur," he says.

"Oh yes. My deceased husband." I recall he died on Monday around sunset. I wasn't with him when it happened. He was late getting home for supper that day. My beef roast was getting too crisp warming in the oven. The ice in the sweet tea had melted.

Then Clyde Willems came and told me Arthur died.

I hear my name called again and look up. "What?"

I stare into a pair of eyes the color of ripe pears.

"Answer my question, Mrs. Powell."

"What question is that?" It's late and the sun has set. I know because through the window I see streetlights casting a yellow glow over the street in front of the police station. I'm so very, very tired.

"Where were you when Arthur passed?" he asks.

"He passed me?" I feel confused. Where was Arthur when he passed me? Was he driving his truck? Did he pass me in my 2008 Cadillac? I don't' recall passing him on Monday, the day he died.

"Mrs. Powell," he says with a tone I don't like, "let's not play games." He shifts in his chair behind his desk and glares at me.

"Games? Oh." I sit up, more alert. "I love games. Do you like Bingo? Because if you do, we play down at the Methodist church every Wednesday afternoon from two to five," I tell him. "Guests are always welcome." Butch has a scowl on his face.

He may be Detective Lloyd Peters to all his peers. But he's plain Butch to me. His mother Susan used to go to First Methodist with me, until she died of a stroke five years ago. No, Butch has no right to scowl at me. I'm the one who's hurting. It was *my* husband that died. "Poor Arthur," I mutter aloud, inapt to function normally.

"Mrs. Powell!" Butch says with force. "You need to focus."

"Are you mad at me, Butch?" I ask. "You brought up the idea of games." I clamp my lips and study the situation. Here I am at the police station trying to be civil to this man, which is hard, trust me.

There's a scowl on Butch's face when we're interrupted.

"Excuse me, Sir?"

I look up and see Ellie Simpson standing in the doorway. I never heard the door open. Must've been daydreaming. I look at the woman good. She's forty-four, I hear. She looks twenty-eight.

I hate her youth, but I despise Butch more.

"What is it, Ellie?" Butch asks as he pushes away from his desk.

Ellie looks at me oddly. Do I have egg on my face? Did I wash up after breakfast? Lord, that seems hours ago. It's Thursday, right?

Three days since Arthur passed. Oh, that was what Butch was talking about when he said Arthur passed. Somehow, I know Ellie's stare is not about egg on my face. She says, "Mrs. Powell's daughter has arrived." And that gets my attention, all right. Big time.

"*My* Claire is here?" I stand up, startled. Of course, she'd want to say goodbye to her daddy. We all want to say goodbye to Arthur.

"Yes, ma'am," Ellie replies to me, sadness in her apple-green eyes.

I'm ready to club Butch, a chip off his sorry daddy's block, if you ask me. He hates people calling him that. My son despised him when they were in high school. *Poor Lance*, he drove a truck for Pict Sweet for thirty years delivering their frozen vegetables till he dropped dead from a heart attack at fifty-one. Too much fat fast food. A body can't eat hamburgers and fries and expect to live till they're my age.

I look hard at Butch. Ellie's still standing there.

"Were you about to say something, Mrs. Powell?"

"Can I see my daughter now?"

Butch says to Ellie, "Tell Claire I'll be out to talk to her first."

"I can't see my daughter right now?" I don't like this at all.

"In a moment, Mrs. Powell." Butch walks to the door. He looks at me once then asks, "Can I get you a Coke while I'm away?"

"Are you going somewhere with my Claire?"

"No. We'll just be outside the door, talking," he says.

"Yes, I'd like a Coke. Please." I mustn't forget my manners.

He shuts the door and leaves me alone.

Alone. Boy, I hate that word. That's what I am now since Arthur has passed. Oh, a light bulb goes off in my silly brain—of course, that was what Butch meant when he asked me the question.

It's Thursday, isn't it?

I forgot my wristwatch. I pat down my frizzy hair and realize I've missed my hair appointment this afternoon at three. Gloria cuts my hair once a month. She works out of her house and only takes cash. She doesn't report all of her income to the IRS. Charges twenty-five dollars for a wash and cut. Highway robbery, ask me.

What's taking Butch and Claire so long?

I feel like a spent penny. The gawdy yellowish light from the pole outside the station shines in my face through the window. I want to get up and close the blinds, but it's not my office.

9

I fidget with the hem of my blouse and wonder what Butch is telling my Claire. Must be something he doesn't want me to hear. I can't imagine what it could be. I'm as honest as Abe Lincoln was.

Ridiculous! I should be talking to Claire. I am her mother.

My hands are shaking. Something doesn't feel right.

What is Butch telling Claire?

I can't just sit here any longer. I walk over to the closed door and lean the side of my face against it so I can hear what they're saying.

My daughter is crying. She misses her daddy.

The door opens and I bump heads with Butch.

He's not happy I was eavesdropping. He's a saucy-kind of detective. Almost fifty and wears his long salt-and-pepper hair in a silly ponytail. A gold stud pierces his right earlobe and his honey-colored eyes are large and expressive for a man. He thinks he's something and knows I don't like him. But his mother Susan was a dear friend. Detective Lloyd Peters will always be Butch to me.

When I look at him, I see scars from teenage pimples. He wears a two-day shadow from not shaving. What do I care? I chuckle to myself at my silliness and accept a cold Coke from Butch.

"Thanks." I glance past him at my lovely daughter.

She sees me looking. "Oh, Mama!"

Claire rushes around Butch and falls into my arms.

"I'm so sorry about Daddy."

She's a limp rag in my sweaty hands but I hug her anyway.

"Don't cry, baby. Arthur is in Heaven," I hear myself say and wonder if it's true. Goodness, I've sat by that man every Sunday at First Methodist for the fifty years, all the time we've owned our farm in Maury County, Tennessee. It never takes Brother Kenny more than ten minutes to put Arthur fast sleep. He doesn't read the Bible or pray aloud. I'm the one who reads *Daily Tip of God's Day.*

"Mama?"

"Yes, Claire."

"Detective Butch says Clyde Willems' found Daddy next to Crystal Creek on Monday," she tells me.

I nod, but my mouth is too dry to speak.

"Has an autopsy been done?"

Claire's question is for Butch. I listen carefully.

"CSI is working on it. We'll have a report soon," he replies.

Poor Arthur. Sliced into little pieces. If I've told him once, I've told him a thousand times, "Don't get on the tractor unless Clyde is with you. You're too blame old to act like a young farmer."

But he never listened.

"Can I go home now, Butch?" I ask him.

He scowls at me. He hates I call him Butch. He waves me off.

Claire intervenes. "Mama's tired, she's still in shock."

"Apparently!" he scowls again, those large eyes haunting me.

I don't appreciate the way Butch treats me. Like it's my fault Arthur died. I was a good wife to him for fifty-six years.

I bore him a son and daughter. *Poor Lance.* I miss my son like he died yesterday. *Poor Arthur.* Clyde found him next to Crystal Creek shortly after sunset on Monday. His tractor was still running.

"Let's go home, Mama." She looks at Butch, daring him to protest. I take her hand and follow her to the door.

It feels like I'm getting out of prison as we go through the open door and past Ellie's desk. I want to shout and praise Jesus!

"Did you have lunch, Mama?"

"No, but I had a late breakfast."

"After supper, we'll have a cup of hot decaf tea so we can sleep better tonight." Claire opens the door leading to the hallway.

"Dorothy?" Butch calls me by my first name.

I pause and turn around.

"Yes, Lloyd?"

I can play his name game, too.

"We haven't finished talking. You understand that, right?"

I sigh, not understanding anything anymore. Why the young die, the old live too long, buzzards eat dead things, bluebirds sing every spring morning. The list of things I don't understand are too long to think about. *Ever!* I try to put one foot in front of the other.

"We'll talk to you tomorrow," Claire tells Butch and I'm tickled to be leaving. I cannot resist looking back and winking one eye.

11

A Time to Be Quiet

2

"WHAT'S WRONG WITH HIM?" I am referring to Detective Peters as Claire and I exit the police station on our way to my Cadillac.

"Nothing's wrong with Butch, he's just doing his job."

I unlock the car doors but Claire is driving. Thunder rumbles and I know a storm is coming our way. She pulls the car into the flow of traffic and we sail far too fast over rolling hills and sharp curves toward my house in the country. But I keep my mouth shut.

I've learned my lesson. The less I say, the better off I am. There are things I've said in certain situations I wish I could delete from history. Regretful statements, especially in light of all that's happened since Monday. But words scatter like confetti in the wind.

"Mama?"

"Yes, Claire." I turn to see her pretty face better.

She looks like I used to when I was approaching fifty. Grandma Lois gave me a set of body genes that I passed on to Claire. Her hair is ruby-red, like Arthur's used to be before he turned bald. Her eyes are the color of a robin's egg. She's a pretty sight to behold.

She turns the curve too fast and the car tires skid.

"Claire!" I scream. "For God's sake, slow down! You don't want Ted to bury three of us from one family, do you?"

Claire eases her foot off the petal and frowns at me.

Maybe, I was a little harsh with her, but the roads are slick from the consistent peppering rain, and the last thing I want is for her to wreck my car and put us in the hospital. But I know I've upset her.

"I didn't mean to scream at you, Claire," I apologize.

"No, Mama. I'm sorry for driving too fast. Like you, I'm stressed out. I need to go to bed early tonight. What time is it?"

I have no idea. After dark, for sure. The windshield wipers are working overtime to wash away the rain and she can't see well.

I squint at the clock built into the dashboard. *No help there*, I forgot it quit working, I forget when. Arthur was going to take my Cadillac to the dealership and get a new clock installed but he never did. I glance at my wrist and realize its missing. *Double S-S!*

I hope it didn't drop off somewhere. The latch needed to be fixed. Hell's bells, I have no idea what time it is.

"I don't know what time it is," I tell Claire.

"Can you get my phone out of my purse?" she asks.

I hear the rain beating like a drum on the roof of the car as I reach in the backseat to get Claire's purse then rummage through it for a cell phone. "How do you turn it on?" I ask.

Let the young folks depend on their electronic contraptions for dates and times, I'm old-fashioned and will stick with a yearly brick-and-mortar wristwatch, or the New Year's calendar that comes in the mail from our insurance company every January.

I laugh at the idea of a brick-and-mortar calendar.

"What's so funny, Mama?"

"Nothing, Claire." She wouldn't understand if I told her.

When the Corona virus invaded America last spring, life changed for a lot of people. Stores closed for months, at least the brick-and-mortar ones. Most younger folks ordered what they needed over the Internet. On-line marketing, they called it. *Why do I care?*

"It's 7:45," I see on the face of the phone.

"No wonder I'm hungry. Do you have food cooked at home?"

She takes another curve too fast and I cringe. My stomach goes woohoo, and a dozen ugly words come to mind, but I say nothing.

"Friends from church came earlier today and left off some casseroles. I forget how many—it's been such a long day."

I use a paper napkin to swipe away the condensation on the windshield as the night turns darker and colder.

"Oh, I forgot I made dump soup yesterday."

It's a yummy delicacy, really easy. Whatever is left over at meals, put in plastic containers and freeze. Later dump everything in the big cooking pot and add a quart of chicken broth and a chopped onion.

Why am I thinking about this now?

13

"Sounds good, I had a light lunch." Claire drives up the long gravel road and pulls under the overhang of the shed fifty feet from my 1890's two-story farmhouse, and shuts off the motor.

We sit there a moment, both in our own world of thoughts. I wonder what Claire will think of me when she learns what I said about her Daddy three days before he fell off his tractor and died?

Secrets are best kept that way.

"We better make a run for the house." Claire opens the door.

I'm grateful the rain has slacked, but it's bitter dark and too cold outdoors for my liking. Peeping through the clouds, the moon is an angry sliver of light that reminds me of a goblin's mouth.

I open the passenger door and climb out. The moist air is saturated with the odor of wet decaying foliage coming from the woods behind the house. I dig into my purse for housekeys and don't find them. "Dadgum it!" I'm frustrated and grumble to myself.

"What's wrong, Mama?" Claire has an umbrella over her head.

I suddenly recall I left my set of keys on the kitchen counter. *Double S-S!!*

Then I recall that Arthur put a housekey under the dead potted Peonies next to the backsteps to our screened porch. *My* screened porch now. Claire stares at me across the hood.

"You seem spacey tonight, Mama."

"I am spacy, Claire. I'm eighty years old, and too blame slow."

Claire manually locks the car.

"You don't have to do that, Arthur and I never do," I say. "Nobody steals this far out." But Claire ignores me and walks across the backyard as I attempt to keep up and fail.

She pulls at the screen door then looks hard at me.

"Tell me you have a key to the screen door."

I feel like she's my mother and I'm her child.

"Under the large pot of dead peonies," I grumble as my shoes sink into the mushy soil. Too dark to see the ground, but I know the grass is turning brown. Arthur meant to plant winter grass but he never got around to it. I chuckle. Like we keep a schedule.

Claire tips my plant and gets the ring with two keys.

My house is a looming shadow shrouded by centuries-old Oaks. For fifty years, Arthur and I have owned this ol' relic sitting on two-hundred acres of rolling Middle Tennessee hills. A distant relative of a Confederate soldier sold us the property. It has history and mystery, a life of its own. *No ghosts, thank God!*

"Which key fits the screen porch?"

I show her and she tries to open it. The key is old and a little rusty and hard to turn. I promise myself I'll get a new copy made.

"Hurry up and open the door!" The cold saturates my bones.

"I'm trying, Mama. Be patient, please."

I've just about spent all my patience in the past three days. The house looking inviting, like it wants me to come inside, tells me I can stay as long as I want. But I've told the walls I have to go one day.

Just like Arthur. Poor Lance.

The screen door opens and I follow Claire across the porch where she uses the other key to let us inside the house. She switches on the kitchen light. "The house smells musky, Mama."

I park my purse on the kitchen table.

"We need to turn on the heat," I decide. "Up until this week, the weather's been pleasant so the systems been shut off."

We're between fall and winter and I'm between, I don't know what I'm between. I sit down at the table and wait while Claire adjusts the thermostat on the den wall. When she returns to the kitchen, I am already removing a big container of vegetable soup from the fridge. I dump the contents in a pot to warm.

"Sit down, Mama, I'll fix our supper."

"Do you remember how to turn on the gas stove?"

Claire sassily parks a hand on one hip, as if disgusted. "Mama, I used to live here. I know how to warm soup over a gas eye."

I clamp my mouth shut. *Double D-D!!* Better I keep it that way.

After supper, Claire washes our bowls and glasses while I dry them with a hand towel, and stow them in their respective cabinets.

I like cleanliness and order. Not much in society is like that these days. A clean house represents a clean heart and a pure soul.

I turn out the lights and we go in the den.

15

"Are you still cold?" Claire asks, though the heat has kicked on.

"We can build a fire, if you like," I suggest. "Arthur has some stacked wood out in the shed if you want to get a few dry logs."

"Sit tight, I'll get enough to build a fire for tonight."

I slouch in the old leather recliner. Arthur's recliner. But he doesn't need it anymore. It reclines and rocks. He bought it eight years ago. My recliner is older and doesn't rock. I like to rock. It comforts my soul. I wait, practicing my patience.

Claire is back in a few minutes and dumps the dry wood in the fireplace, adds a wad of old newspapers, then torches the stack with a long match. Soon, heat leaps from the fiery hearth.

"I'd like a cup of hot decaf tea," Claire says. "You want some."

"Sure." I stare into the leaping flames that look like demons dancing on the crackling wood. If evil spirits are real, I wonder if they laugh at people. I linger in my thoughts until Claire returns.

"Here, Mama." Claire hands me my cup.

"Peppermint?" I smell the honey-colored liquid.

"Yes," she says, sighs, and collapses on the green corduroy sofa.

We sit for a while. It's 8:45 p.m. by the wall clock. If Arthur were here, he'd be preparing for bed. He gets up at five a.m. every morning to milk our one pitiful cow. I tell him all the time at breakfast that Kroger has good milk we can buy. That he's too blamed old to get up so early in the morning and milk a stupid cow.

"Mama?"

"Yes?" I look at my daughter.

"What did Detective Peters want with you?"

"Butch?" I threw a hand. "We talked and really said nothing."

"Did he ask specific questions?"

I shrug because I don't want to talk about it.

"Lloyd seemed pretty upset when he came out to talk to me," Claire recalls. "What did he mean by we're not through talking?"

Goodness, Claire is as bad as Butch.

"He's always had his tail in a twist," I say. "Susan used to say he'd never amount to much. I guess being a detective puts a star on his cap." I slowly sip my tea and stare into the demonic flames.

16

"Okay." Claire's lips fold into her mouth. "I tried talking to you on the phone Monday, right after Clyde told you Daddy died."

"You did?" *Monday night is a fog to me.*

"You called me, Mama. Remember?"

"Monday night is sketchy in my mind," I say.

"Okay, maybe by tomorrow you'll feel more like sharing. While I'm here, we need to tend to some business."

Claire studies me with her clear-blue eyes.

"What kind of business?"

"Tomorrow, we're going to the bank and get Daddy's life insurance policy out of the lockbox and any other documents we might need," Claire says. "We'll also need his birth certificate. You'll have to cancel everything in his name, like his social security card."

Claire stares through me like I'm not sitting three feet from her.

"Is there anything important you need to tell me, Mama?"

I bite my lip. *Oh, Lord, I was afraid she would ask me that.*

"You know you can tell me anything, I'm on your side and I always will be." She reaches over to grasp my hand.

"Well," I gather courage, "I may have said something I ought not have said. Some folks might not take it like I meant it."

Claire looks horrified. "Mama. What did you say and to whom?"

To whom. Now, that's a city girl's response. Claire is married to Theodore Harold Burkes the Third, a brilliant attorney. They use *perfect* English, have *perfect* children, *perfect* friends, and a home far more *perfect* than mine. *I don't want to talk about what I said.*

"Mama." Claire snaps her fingers. "What did you say and to whom?" She is relentless and will not let this question go.

"Well, I sometimes say things at the Mary Martha Circle meeting I shouldn't." *But that's not the time I'm talking about.*

"What things, Mama?"

"You know, our circle meets at the church every third Tuesday of the month and have a potluck lunch afterwards. Beverly Brown was in charge of the October program. Since she plants a huge flower garden in the spring, she invited a beekeeper to tell us what kind of plants feed the little critters during the fall months." *I'm on a roll to never disclose*

17

what Lorene Perkins and I said last Friday when we played cards from two till five at the Senior Citizen Center.

"Mama, stay focused. Did you say anything about Daddy?"

"Sort of." I shouldn't have opened up that can of worms so close to bedtime. If I go over all that, I might not get a drop of sleep.

"Mama?"

"Yes, dear?"

"Who did you sort of say something to someone you ought not should have said?" Claire tries to repeat my words and it tickles me.

"Nothing is funny, Mama. Daddy is dead."

"I wasn't laughing at Arthur," I take exception.

"Just tell me what you said and the person you said it to."

"I—" Claire's cell phone rings. *Saved by the bell.*

"Hold that thought, Mama, I need to take this."

Claire disappears into the kitchen and I breathe easier. It's 9:32 by the wall clock. I'm sleepy. I move over to the sofa, lay down and close my eyes. Everything that's happened fades into nothingness.

A Time to Find

3

Friday, October 29th

SUNLIGHT TRICKLES THROUGH the window blinds as I wake up Friday morning. Late Monday, I learned Arthur had died. I missed my hair appointment with Gloria yesterday and my head itches.

I should wash my hair today.

"Mama?"

I realize I smell bacon cooking. I glance toward the kitchen. Claire is standing in the archway fully dressed for the day.

"Good morning, Mama," she says with a smile.

"Did I sleep all night on the sofa?" I ask.

"Yes, like a log," she replies.

Yesterday is a fog to me. I try to recall last night.

"Ted called. We talked a good while. When I returned to the den you were asleep. I covered you with an afghan and let you be."

I sit up and feel stiff. Old bones, sore muscles. I yawn. "Did you make breakfast for us?" I struggle to stand up.

Rheumatoid is relentlessly my archenemy.

I try to keep my balance as I walk into my lovely kitchen. Its ceilings are high and the old wooden floors feel solid beneath my unsteady feet. Early nineteenth-century homes are like that. Arthur put up new wallpaper last year. A chicken and floral print.

Claire has set the table with my ceramic breakfast china. Arthur and I always use the Corelle for breakfast. I sit down in a chair, silent with my scattered thoughts, and expect Claire to serve me.

She sets two plates of food on the table. Mine has scrambled eggs, two slices of bacon, and a piece of toast slathered in butter.

I usually have cereal or instant oatmeal. She's having yogurt and canned mixed fruit. *Boring.* I look at my lovely daughter. She wears a size six pants and an eight blouse. Busty, like I am.

"Thanks for making breakfast, Claire."

We eat in silence as the sun brings light to the kitchen. I think about life in general. Some things never seem to change. I've saved a lot of things, but you can't save time. It's like a rollercoaster on a track to nowhere. Every circle you pass puts age and wrinkles on you. And sometimes misery. And always death. Always.

"Mama?" Claire draws my attention to the present.

I realize she's finished eating and I haven't touched my food.

"Yes, dear." I try to open my bleary blue eyes wider.

"After we finish breakfast, Mama, you need to take a shower and wash your hair. I'll blow it dry and use my hot iron to tame the curls," she offers. "I'm sorry you missed your hair appointment."

"Don't worry!" I huff. "Gloria makes plenty of money off me. She knows I'll be back to her house again." I'm in a complaining mood as Claire gathers our dirty dishes and takes them to the sink.

I'm not hungry, so why eat?

I can tell I've upset Claire. She bangs the pots and pans as she washes them and lets them dry in the metal drainer.

"I'm sorry I'm in such a mood," I apologize.

"It's okay, Mama, I know you're upset. And you have a right to be. It hasn't been a good week for either of us."

"Thank you for understanding."

"Now, you need to get dressed so we can be at First Federal Bank when it opens at nine." Claire dries her hands and ventures into the den. "I need to see what's inside Daddy's lockbox."

We all *need* something. Our stares are locked and loaded.

Am I ready for this?

"Do you have a key to Daddy's lockbox?"

"Oh, Lordy!" I declare. "Somewhere, I'll have to look for it."

In a tizzy, I rush through the den, tramp down the hall and enter our bedroom. *My* bedroom, I correct myself. By the time Claire catches up with me, I'm going through the dresser drawers.

Now, where would Arthur hide a lockbox key?

Then I remember there's a big keepsake box at the top of the closet. It might be there. I get a stool and prop it next to a sturdy chair. "Mama, please don't climb upon that chair, you might fall."

20

Too late, I'm already halfway up and about to ground my feet on the seat of the chair. It wobbles as I successfully climb up.

I reach up high and snag the corner of the floral box.

"Hand it down to me, Mama! Don't you dare try to climb down while holding it," Claire orders, a little too harshly in my own mind.

Does she think I am an old fool? I've climbed upon chairs since I was two years old. But I hand her the box anyhow.

Hell's bells, I don't feel like arguing this morning.

Claire opens the box while I slowly climb down.

"You think Daddy's lockbox key is in here?"

She thumbs through dozens of old pictures I've failed to put in an album. Exasperated, she sets the box on the floor.

"Mama, go take a shower and wash your hair. I'll dump all of this, uh, stuff, on the bed and go through it. It's 8:15 already."

The bathroom is off the hall between my bedroom and the guest's. Old houses weren't built with master baths. I always wanted one installed in our bedroom, but Arthur said additions to historic houses would be detrimental if we ever decided to sell.

When I finish showering, I return to my bedroom, briskly toweling my kinky white curls. I might have a blond color put on now that Arthur has no say-so in the matter. He hates old women with colored hair. He said it makes the face show more wrinkles.

I don't know about Arthur, what does he know about hair? He had none when he passed out of this troubled world.

"The key wasn't in the box," Claire reports, her lips twisted.

Then I remember Arthur keeps the key locked in his truck, like I'm going to borrow it for any reason under the sun.

"I know where it is," I say with mental clarity.

Claire turns on the hairdryer as I sit in the chair at my antique dresser, the same chair I used to climb upon to reach the shelf in the closet to get the box that had nothing useful in it.

Double S-S! I say to wasted time. *Time, I don't have.*

"There, all dry and pressed, Mama. Get dressed and let's go."

Claire leaves me alone in the bedroom as I pick out a bright pink pantsuit with a floral scarf. I don't want to wear black. I'm a widow, not a black widow like the spider that killed the man she once loved.

It was a dumb thought. I hurriedly dressed as Claire is already outside and honking her car horn for me to hurry. I grab a large sweater from my closet and put it on then toddle into the den. I see though the window that Claire's is backing up and turning around.

I don't do hurry easily. My walk is unsteady and my heart beats hard when I rush. Still I lock the backdoor and hurry to the car.

"What's the rush, Claire? We've got all day!"

"Mr. Hornsby doesn't," she tells me. "Get in the car, Mama. We have a nine o'clock appointment. He's personally letting us into the vault to open Daddy's lockbox." She shows me the key.

"I was right?" I haven't lost all my marbles, thank God!

"Yes, you were. The key was locked in the glove compartment of Daddy's old Ford pickup." She starts the Buick's motor.

Oh, goody! We're off to see the Wizard.

I stare at the trees passing the car as we roll down my long gravel driveway and past the mailbox. Once on the main highway, it takes only twenty minutes to reach town. Columbia, Tennessee is exactly ten miles from our property. Decades ago, Arthur cleared some acreage to plant hay and graze a dozen cows. Two years ago, there were only four left. Three more died last winter. We're down to one milk cow that lives in the barn two-hundred feet from the house.

"You're mighty quiet this morning, Mama," Claire says to me as we enter the bank through the front door. "We're here to see Mr. Hornsby," Claire tells a young bank teller with purple hair.

Lucy Brown is new. What is she, twenty if a day?

"Have a seat, Claire. You, too, Mrs. Powell," Carl says.

Like I'm second in line. *You, too?* Really? I sit down and say nothing. Claire is in charge today. I'm keeping my mouth shut.

Claire looks at me then addresses Carl. "Detective Peters mentioned Daddy has a life-insurance policy," she tells him.

I sit up erect, surprised.

"Arthur took out a life-insurance policy?"

Claire pats my hand. To Carl, she says. "Please let us in my daddy's lockbox so we can find the policy." She hands him the key.

He stands up and grins like a fox. "Follow me."

King of the roost! All the way from pumping gas at the Exxon Station to bank manager. Somebody in town has strings to pull.

We're inside the vault and the door is locked. I'm hot as Claire removes the paperwork from the lockbox and thumbs through it.

"Here, it is!" She shows the envelope to me. "And," she holds up a paper in her other hand, "Here is Daddy's birth certificate."

"What about his will-and-testament?" I ask.

Claire hands me the two docs while she finds Arthur's will.

"Here is it, Mama. Everything we need for your attorney." She closes the metal box and shoves it in the pocket of the stand-up safe.

Oh, goody! One thing accomplished today.

"Let's go back home and see what we have."

"Can we stop by Dunkin Donuts first? I have a gift card." I want a large hazelnut latte with whipped cream.

"Okay, Mama, no problem." She aims to please me.

Dunkin is busy as usual, but our time arrives as we trundle with the slow drive-through traffic. Claire turns down coffee.

Not me. I have too much to face today without my caffeine fix.

"One medium hazelnut latte, hot," she tells the speaker.

And we are on our way to wherever today takes us.

"Claire, can we talk to Butch another day?" I ask, relishing my first sip of coffee, as if it were a friend, or a nice relative, or Arthur, but never forsakes me. I am as looney as a cartoon character.

"I suppose the conversation with Detective Peters can wait another time," Claire agrees. "Anyhow, I prefer to review these documents before we revisit the police station."

Oh goody! I already feel better.

We're in the car driving too fast toward home when Claire looks over and asks, "Have you spoken to Lorene Perkins this week?"

"No. I'm surprised she hasn't called me."

"Do you know her husband, Crawford?"

"Arthur's Poker buddy? Not well, why?"

"The Perkins attend First Baptist Church, and I play cards with Lorene at the Senior Citizen Center every Friday afternoon from two to five," I inform Claire, knowing I won't be there this week.

I wonder who will take my place.

"How well do you know her?"

"We've been friends for as long as I can remember. The Perkins built that huge brick home on Simpson Road," I inform Claire. "Arthur and Clyde Willems play Poker with Crawford and five other guys twice a month on Fridays. Bubba's a barber. Jimmy is a lawyer. And—" Claire interrupts me. "I don't need to know the names of Daddy's poker friends. We were discussing Lorene. Okay?"

"What about Lorene?" I feel strange at the question.

"Detective Peters told me Lorene's husband also died on Monday." Claire's eyes are on me like fleas on a dog.

"What?" I ponder the news. "Did he have a heart attack?"

"I don't know the details, Mama, but Detective Peters thinks it odd that both Daddy and Crawford died on the same day."

"I admit it's hugely strange."

"He's suspicious their deaths aren't natural."

I shrug, feeling somehow intimidated. "All deaths are natural, Claire. It's natural to be born. Natural to grow up, date, and get married. Natural to have children then grandchildren then get old and then die. It was Crawford's time, that's all it was."

We don't talk again until we get home.

First thing, I go out to the shed to see if Arthur left anything out there that I should bring into the house. I open the door and stare into the darkness then switch on a light. In the middle of an empty space on the floor there's a large wrench with some red mud on it. I pick it up and lay it on the rough wooden shelf where Arthur measures out meds for the cow. I close up and trek to the house.

In the kitchen, I notice the documents from the lockbox are displayed on the breakfast table. Claire is reading Arthur's will.

Without looking up, she sips from a glass of sweet tea.

Feeling I'm there, she looks up.

"Find anything useful in the shed?"

"No. Anything unusual in those papers?" I ask.

"Do you want to read Daddy's will?"

"I know what's in it. I get the farm and the bank account—which I'm afraid is not worth much. We've pretty much lived off our social security a while. Arthur cashed in all our stocks a decade ago."

Claire hands me Arthur's will anyhow. I glance at it then lay it down and try to remember how I felt when my daddy died.

"You are a wealthy widow, Mama!" she exclaims.

I blink. "Who, me?" My hands tremble at her statement.

"And you never knew that Daddy took out a five-hundred-thousand-dollar life insurance policy on himself two years ago?"

"Double S-S. No!" I exclaim, flabbergasted.

"Now, Mama, you don't have to curse."

"I didn't." But she knows what I mean. S is for manure and D stands for a wall of brick that holds back water. Good Methodists don't curse. I stare at my daughter, speechless.

"I can see this news upsets you. Let's drive back into town and I'll buy you lunch. Then we'll drop off Daddy's will at Attorney Jacob Dunwoody's office. Then we should revisit the police station so Detective Peters can finish asking you his questions."

I look at Claire. "Am I in trouble?"

Claire smacks her lips. "Let's see what the autopsy shows."

"Arthur's autopsy," I conclude.

"And Crawford Perkins," Claire reveals.

"What has Crawford's death got to do with Arthur's?"

"I don't know, but I'm sure Detective Peters will find out."

"Do I need a lawyer?" I ask.

"You might, but Ted can handle anything that comes up," Claire says. "Meanwhile, I don't want you worry. We'll figure out things."

Things. I let what things marinate in my thoughts.

"Oh, dear Lord!" My hands fly to my mouth. "Do you think Butch knows about the life-insurance policy? He probably thinks I did it for the *D-D* money!" I curse and don't care that I am a Methodist.

A Time to Interview

4

LATE MORNING FRIDAY, Detective Lloyd Peters has Clyde Willems in his office interviewing him concerning Arthur Powell's death.

"Were you and Arthur friends?" Lloyd inquires.

"Yes, but I was his field hand. We didn't have the same living standards." Clyde feels uncomfortable inside the police station.

"Does that bother you?" Lloyd inquires.

"What? That I was Arthur's field hand?"

"No, that Arthur lived better than you did," Lloyd says.

"No, I respected Arthur, he treated me like a true friend."

"Tell me how you feel about his death," Lloyd says.

"Well, I feel like Arthur was plucked out of the Great Garden of Life too soon." Clyde gulps back tears. "That's how I feel, Butch."

Detective Peters cringes. Everybody who knows him in town calls him Butch. Even after he'd finished college and attended the Police Academy in Nashville, they disrespect him. He doesn't know why they can't recognize his important position in the community.

"That's real poetic, Clyde." Lloyd reins in his temper.

"Can I go now? I need to finish cutting the field Arthur didn't get to on Monday," Clyde says. "What else do you want to know?"

"You said you found him lying on the bank of Crystal Creek."

"Yes, sir, I did. He was turned on his stomach with the back of his head bleeding. I didn't touch him, just got on my four-wheel and rode over to his house to tell Dorothy about Arthur."

"Were you sure he was dead?"

"Yep, his eyes were open and staring."

"Exactly what time did you discover Arthur's body?"

"Eight o'clock sharp. I know because I was gonna miss my favorite show on television, CSI Las Vegas. You ever watch that program?" Clyde glares though muddy-brown eyes.

"Sometimes," Lloyd replies. "Do you gamble, Clyde?"

"Yeah. Eight of us boys meet twice a month on a Friday evening to play Poker." He looks at Butch. "Is that important?"

"Just trying to learn what I can about the players," Lloyd replies.

"So, you can play Poker with us?" Clyde scratches his head.

Lloyd winks a smile. "I was referring to the people who know Arthur best and are around him often," Lloyd explains.

"Oh." Clyde looks away, embarrassed.

"Tell me how Arthur's wife reacted when you told her what had happened to him?" Lloyd assessed Clyde's truthfulness.

"Oh, she was powerfully upset."

"Did Dorothy say anything specific?"

"Nope, just stumbled back a few steps. I kept her from falling and helped her in the den so she could sit a spell."

"That was good, Clyde. Very kind of you," Lloyd says.

"I always liked Arthur. He was a good friend, though he lived a lot better than I did," Clyde jaws, probably talking too much.

Lloyd frowns while tapping his ballpoint pen on his desk.

"What? I say something wrong, Detective?"

"Clyde? Were you jealous of Arthur's wealth?"

"No, sir, it wasn't like that. He had a nicer place to live than I did, didn't owe nobody money. Paid me well for my help. He was always good to me, helped me out if I ever got in a bind."

"Do you often get in a bind, Clyde?" Lloyd probes.

"Ever' body sometimes gets in a bind, Butch."

Lloyd cringes and wants to reach across his desk and slap some sense into Clyde Willems. Instead, he presses on with his job.

"Okay. When did you leave Arthur's house Monday evening?"

"I hung around a spell, had a cup of coffee while Ms. Powell called her daughter to tell her about Arthur. I left around 9:15."

"Okay, then." Lloyd lays his notepad aside.

"Okay, what?"

"You can go back to work now," Lloyd says.

"Okay, then." Clyde grabs his straw hat and scoots out of the office, grateful to put the law as far from him as possible.

* * *

"Wasn't that Clyde Willems getting in his truck?" Claire asks.

It's nearly one p.m. And we are back at the police station.

"Where?" I stretch my neck to see out the rear window and catch a glimpse of an old blue truck pulling out on Third Street.

"It looks like Clyde's pickup," Claire says as she parks in the handicapped space for visitors and kills the motor to my Cadillac.

Doc Hammons wrote me a prescription for one of those old folks' tags you put on the front window so you can park and not have to walk so far to get into a building. The motor grows quiet.

Claire turns in her seat to face me. "Mama?"

"Yes, dear?" I know that serious look.

"I want you to answer Detective Peter's questions honestly but don't volunteer anything extra. Understand?"

Her blue eyes haunt me, but I can't let on I'm scared.

"Okay. Jus' the facts, ma'am." I open the car door and get out.

Inside the station, Claire tells Ellie why we're here.

We wait. Five minutes doesn't pass before Detective Butch comes out of his office all dressed up in spiffy gray slacks, and a plaid shirt he probably ordered online from one of those fancy stores.

He motions for us to join him in his office then closes the door.

I feel like I'm locked up in jail. I remember what Claire said: *Just the facts*. I notice two vacant chairs are positioned in front of Butch's wood and chrome desk. I sit in one and Claire takes the other.

"I brought Mama to answer your questions."

"Thank you, Claire."

He looks at my daughter like he could eat her. I knew Butch was sweet on Claire when she was a freshman in high school and he was a senior. I don't trust him, even now. Theodore better get his butt to town before Butch makes his pitch and asks Claire out.

Most people think I'm naïve. I'm not. I know couples aren't always faithful to their marriage vows. I see it with my own eyes.

Butch sits down at his desk and laces his fingers together on the shiny surface of his desk. I think he works out at the gym more than he solves crimes—not that anything serious happens in our part of Tennessee. Mostly, it's Nashville where murders are common.

I take in a breath, already anxious to leave.

"You were right, Detective Peters," Claire says as she hands him Arthur's life-insurance policy. "Mama is the sole beneficiary of half a million dollars upon Daddy's death." She waits for his response.

Butch taps the folder on his desk three times and looks at me with those Mellow Yellow eyes that remind me of puke and make me want to vomit. I can see him winding up to ask me a question.

"Mrs. Powell, were you with Arthur when he took out this large insurance policy?" He stares a hole through my face and I hate it.

"No," I reply. "I didn't know until today when Claire told me."

"Were you and Arthur on good terms before he died?"

"As good of terms as any couple that's lived together for fifty-six years," I tell him. "Yes, we argued sometimes, and we both may have said some things we were sorry for, but I can tell you making up is so much better." I think of sex with Arthur and actually blush.

Claire looks at me as if a thought has flashed in her mind.

"Mama, what did you say to someone you shouldn't have said?"

Oh, Lordy! We are back to that subject again. If words were stones, I'm be throwing them as far away from me as I could.

A Time to Grieve

5

AFTER WE FINISH UP at the police station, Claire drives us home.

Her husband Theodore has come for a visit. His Mercedes Benz is parked in the driveway so Claire drives around it and pulls my 2004 Cadillac under the shed overhang. We get out and I'm reminded that the grass needs cutting. "Did you know he was coming?"

"Ted said he might drive up for the weekend."

We wade across tall dead grass that's bowed as if on its knees praying. The ground beneath my feet feels wet and spongy from last night's rain. Claire opens the screen door and we cross the porch and enter my kitchen. Theodore stands there, still wearing his suit.

"Hey, honey," she says and they hug.

He's a smart attorney and always dresses the part. Out here in the country, he should replace those duds with a pair of blue jeans and relax a bit, but who am I to tell him that? I'm his mother-in-law.

Theodore gives me a loose hug. "We're so sorry about Arthur. He was such a good guy," he says. What is this WE? Isn't he sorry?

"Thank you, Theodore, it's been a rough week." I see he's warmed up my soup and already eaten because his dirty bowl has been left in the sink for me to wash. "Did you get dessert?"

"No, I didn't see anything set out," he replies.

"Claire, would you like a bowl of ice cream with chocolate syrup topped with pecans?" We had takeout from Wendy's in Columbia.

"Sure, Mama." She sheds her coat.

"I'm sure Ted will enjoy Blue Bell Homemade Vanilla."

Claire removes three white ceramic bowls from the kitchen cabinet while I get the ice cream out of the fridge freezer.

In the next few minutes, we're seated at the table eating.

Theodore finishes his ice cream first. He's a little overweight, but still had his brown hair. Arthur started losing his when he was barely thirty. I always wanted him to get a wig to cover the bald spots but he refused. Oh, well, I finish eating my dessert.

"Honey," Claire says sweetly to Theodore, "did you bring in your bag yet?" I can see she's still all moony-eyed over him. I expect they have a good sex life. But who am I to ask? I'm the mother and the mother-in-law. And frankly, it's none of my damn business.

Did I just think that? Shame on me.

"I want to see the crime scene," Theodore says.

"What crime scene?" I take exception to his remark.

"Where Arthur died, down by the creek," he explains.

"It wasn't a crime. Arthur fell off his tractor and hit his head," I say. "That's all there is to it. We'll bury him next week and not talk about it again." I feel like cracking a brick on my knee, if I could.

"Mama!!" Claire is horrified.

I sit down and put my head in my hands.

"I'm sorry, I'm so sorry. I can't take this anymore. I've had enough talk of death! My time is coming soon and I don't want to think about somebody finding my body lying beside a creek or in this old house where I've lain for three days and stink like a dead cow."

I sit up and look at Claire and her husband.

Did I just say that?

"I think Mama needs some time alone to grieve," Claire tells Theodore. "Why don't we take a walk. It's about a half mile to where Crystal Creek runs through the property." Claire looks at me.

"You go ahead, I'm going to lie down and rest."

"Will you be okay?"

"Alone, you mean?" I nod my head.

When they leave, I grab my list of phone numbers and call Lorene Perkins on my landline. It rings four times and I wonder if she's home from the Senior Citizen Center yet.

But I hear a bleak hello as someone answers.

"Is Lorene there?" I ask.

"It's me, Claire."

"Oh, I didn't recognize your voice at first," I say.

"I know Arthur died the same day as Crawford. Don't you think that's strange?" She falls silent and mutters to herself.

"Lorene?"

"Did you just say something to me?"

"Did you tell anyone else what we said to Lizzy and Jane last Friday when we were playing cards at the Senior Citizen Center?"

"No, did you?"

"No way." I cover the receiver with a hand as if God is listening. "We cannot mention it to anybody. Are we clear?"

"As a bell!"

"Good." I'm agreeable as the men who signed the Declaration of Independence. "I'm sorry to hear Crawford passed."

"And I'm sorry Arthur died," Lorene says.

"I guess the Poker boys will replace them with two younger studs from town." I feel like bawling, but I must stay strong.

"Crawford always liked Arthur. They took out life-insurance policies at the same time, two years ago. Did you know that?"

"Not until Claire told me," I answer. "First time I laid eyes on it was at the bank when Claire took it out of the safety lockbox."

I can't imagine why Arthur didn't tell me.

"I think it looks bad," Lorene says.

"What do you mean?"

"Well, we aren't exactly poor now that our husbands are dead."

"And if anyone remembers what we said last week when we played cards at the Center, we could be in big trouble."

"We loved our husbands," Lorene says.

"Yes, but . . ."

"But what?" Lorene startles.

"What if Detective Butch thinks otherwise?"

"You think he's thinks we planned to murder our husbands so we could get the insurance money? That's hysterical!"

"I know, we're both Christians!" I noticed the clothes basket sitting at my feet filled with dirty towels and Arthur's work clothes.

"I need to wash clothes, Lorene," I tell her.

"Okay, do that. But keep in touch, friend."

"Wait! Did you play cards this afternoon?"

"No, did you?" Lorene asks.

"No, I wonder who took our places."

"Some younger girls, I expect."

"I hope not forever," I say and it depresses me.

"Have a good rest of the day," Lorene says.

The call ends and I haul the clothes basket to the laundry room. A few minutes later, my old washer is grinding out the dirt.

Claire and Theodore have been gone for over an hour. I am folding Arthur's clean work clothes when I hear the back door open. They're back from their walk. "I'm in the den, reading my Bible."

"It's started to drizzle rain," Theodore comments then shakes water from his thinning brown hair. "I expect it will turn colder."

"Mama, do I need to thaw out anything for supper tonight?"

"Oh, Lordy! I forgot all about supper."

I jump up from Arthur's recliner, thinking I'm going to call it mine now since he doesn't need it.

"I'll see what's in the refrigerator," Claire offers.

Theodore sits down at the breakfast table reviewing the headlines in the *Daily News Journal.* "Stock market's down from the Covid-19 virus scare." He flips the paper over to see the ads.

"I'm not going to worry about a little bug killing me," I tell him. "When it's my time, God will know it and He'll come get me."

Theodore shrugs and continues reading.

"There are two casseroles and four T-bone steaks in the freezer," Claire reports. "Let's thaw out three steaks. Ted can grill them on the back porch for us and I'll nuke three potatoes."

"There's shredded cheese and sour cream in the fridge," I say.

"We should be fine for supper, but I'll need to grocery shop tomorrow." Claire takes care of supper preparations.

Time passes before Claire sets the table.

I inquire about my grandchildren, what they're up to these days. Helen is twenty-six, married, with two pre-school children. She's an RN and works for Vanderbilt Hospital. Benjamin, four years younger, is following in his father's footsteps and studying to become a lawyer. Theodore represents several popular country-western music artists.

I expect he makes a lucrative salary.

"Ben's still single," Claire offers. "If he has a girlfriend, he's not telling us." I worry Benjamin will never marry and shack up with some girl with no morals. No church background and no family ties.

I sigh over the dreadful idea.

It's dark by five o'clock. Day Light Saving Time doesn't save much light at the end of the day. I hate the gloomy darkness that descends over Tennessee during winter months. I miss Arthur.

Theodore burns the steaks—that's what he calls it. And Claire nukes the potatoes. I'm the butter-and-sour-cream champion.

We watch a movie on the Hallmark channel and go to bed early.

I bear my grief privately. I want to scream and cry out to God and ask Him why Arthur died and left me behind. I don't like living alone. I don't know what will happen to me tomorrow, the next day, the next week, the next month, or the next year. So, I lay in bed repeating the Lord's Prayer over and over again till I fall asleep.

A Time for Hating

6

Saturday, October 30th

"TED, WHILE YOU CATCH up on business calls, I'm taking Mama to town to get groceries. I've made a list of the items she needs."

"Okay, honey. It's a nice sunny day, enjoy your trip."

It might not be a nice day for me, depending on what happens with Arthur. I hate thinking about death, it depresses me. I stand in the middle of my den like a Dodo bird afraid to move.

"Mama, are you ready to go?" Claire asks.

"Oh. Yes. I need to get my purse from my bedroom. Will I need my checkbook?" I look to Claire because I suspect we'll do more than grocery shop. She's mentioned the funeral home.

Theodore is correct, it's pleasant outdoors. The gentle wind whisks the rest of the leaves from the limbs of the deciduous trees.

Imagine me knowing the difference between a Conifer and a deciduous tree. I actually once taught Biology at the high school.

Lordy! That was fifteen years ago. *Time is no friend of mine.*

We get in my Cadillac and Claire will drive. She backs into the road in front of my yard as I manually crack my window.

"You want to do that, Mama? It's pretty cool outside."

"It's only a little crack, and I need fresh air to breathe better."

When the electronics went out on my Cadillac sometime back, I had manual windows and doors installed. The repairman tried to talk me out of it, but I insisted. I fear driving off the road into a lake and drowning. I want windows that work when I want them to.

"You're mighty quiet, Mama." Claire says as she takes a curve far too fast for my comfort. "Are you ready for this?"

"Ready for what?" I look out the window. The weatherman reported it would be sixty-five degrees by the middle of the day.

"To pick out Daddy's urn," she replies.

"You mean his casket." I refuse to hyperventilate over the trauma Claire is about to put me through. She says we're grocery shopping, but I knew there is more to our trip than that.

"No, Mama. Daddy has been, uh," she falls silent.

"Just say it, Claire!" My anger shows. "Butch sent his body to the butcher to chop him up in little pieces! I. Get. It."

I sob and hate myself for losing control.

"Mama?" Claire takes her hand off the wheel to pat mine. "I can do this alone if you're not up to it. Daddy will be cremated."

I look at her with tears in my eyes.

"No, Claire, it's my job as Arthur's widow."

Arthur and I dated in high school. He attended Tennessee Tech and majored in Wild Life Management. For years, he worked as a Soil Conservation specialist, advising farmers how to plant the right grasses to feed their wildlife. He was reliable and trusted.

I attended Tennessee Tech and majored in Biology. My first job was teaching at Dickson High School. I never had a serious beau until I was twenty-three, when I ran into Arthur at a birthday party for a mutual friend. He was so good looking and personable.

He swept me off my feet. I recall all those times we parked in his new green Ford truck on a lonely county road and almost went all-the-way. If I ever did, I knew my mama would *kill* me.

I gulp and jerk at my stunning thought.

"What's wrong, Mama? Are you having a stroke?"

I laugh so hard, despite myself.

"No, dear. Just a private thought."

I recall my promise to Lorene. We must not tell anyone about our comment the last time we played cards at the Senior Citizen Center. We can only hope Jane Murphy and Elizabeth *big-mouth* Hinson have not repeated our words. Lizzy is in my Sunday School Class at First Methodist, but she's prone to gossip and speculates on practically every topic imaginable. She was getting a cold the last time I saw her. I should call and see how she is feeling.

Claire pulls into Johnson's Funeral Home and parks out back.

I don't see but a few cars. A black hearse is parked under the side portico in preparation of an upcoming funeral. I wonder if Crawford Perkins' body in in one of the visitation rooms.

The motor grows silent and we sit there. I wish Susan Peters was still alive so I could talk to her about her son Butch, feel her out for what he thinks about Arthur's death. I know he despises me.

"Mama, let's get out, go inside, and get this over with."

I shrug and manually open my door to get out of the car.

We walk to the portico, past the black hearse, and enter a side door to the funeral home. It smells like potpourri, too cold for my old bones. I hate it here. It reminds me of when my parents died.

And poor Lance. He looked so young in his coffin.

I wonder what people will think of me when they view my dead body in a shiny new casket. I sincerely hope Butch doesn't have CSI butcher me. I trail Claire down the long hallway to the main office.

Blake Johnson, the former owner's grandson, runs the funeral home now. His father, Grayson Johnson, has been dead for twenty years. Arthur and I attended his funeral. We viewed him in the most expensive casket available for purchase. Grayson looked nice in his black suit. His eyes were closed but I knew they were brown.

"We're here to talk to Blake," Claire tells his secretary.

I wait, linger, then want to run away from my responsibility. This is killing me, but I don't want to show it. I'm strong, I want folks to believe. "He'll be with you momentarily," Rachel says.

I think about momentarily. Momentarily is a week ago on Saturday, when Arthur and I had just finished a late breakfast. We made love, imagine that. But there's meds for difficult activities.

I smile to myself.

"Did you have a pleasant thought, Mama?"

"Yes, Claire. It was *real* pleasant." I glow with the memory.

The door to the inner office comes open and Blake stands there.

"Claire. Mrs. Powell. Please come in."

Says the spider to the flies. But we go inside anyway.

"I suppose you are here to plan Arthur's funeral," Blake says so matter-of-factly I want to club him. What does this whippersnapper know about death? Or grief, for that matter?

"Please have a seat," he tells us.

I glance around his office. Too perfect. Everything is ruby-red velvet and plush. The carpet in a dark-green tweed pattern. The ceilings are tall with walls wearing embossed-floral paper. This was once a mansion on Main Street Columbia, built during the Civil War.

But now it's a Grieving Hostel where folks that lost loved ones can come and say their final goodbyes. I gulp back my tears.

"How do you suggest we bury Arthur?" I ask Blake.

"Well, considering he's been autopsied, I suggest cremation."

"That's my thought, too," Claire says. "Can we see your urns?"

"I need to use the restroom first," I tell them, then step out in the drab cold hallway and race down to the Women's Restroom so they won't see me create a scene. I close the door behind me and let out a scream. I flush the commode as Claire explodes into the bathroom without knocking and looks at me like I've lost my mind.

"Mama! Was that you screaming? Are you okay?"

I stand up, though a bit wobbly.

"Yes, I screamed. NO, I'm not okay. Yes, I'm going to pick out a nice colorful urn for poor Arthur. We will set a time for a memorial service, leave here and go grocery shopping, then go home and try to forget this day ever happened. Are we CLEAR?"

"As a bell, Mama."

I smile and hug my daughter. She's so precious.

The task doesn't take longer than thirty minutes. We were in Kroger for another forty minutes. I paid the bill by check and Claire drove home. We passed four cars I didn't recognize.

"Was that Detective Peters driving the last car?" Claire asks.

"I didn't see him." I wonder if he came out to the house to ask me more questions. We don't say much as we sail down the highway.

Claire pulls under the shed's overhang, turns off the motor and we get out of my Cadillac. I can't count the number of times I've walked across this yard to my back porch. The dew on the grass has dissipated with sunlight. Theodore opens the kitchen door for us.

Claire's husband doesn't look happy.

We go inside and shed our jackets.

"Dorothy, perhaps you should sit down."

I was all on board with that because I was weary. Both the trip, and from thinking about Arthur's burial. "Did the world end?"

I'm in no mood for bad news, no ma'am.

"Please have a seat." He locks eyes with Claire. "Both of you."

We go into the den and sit down. I choose to sit in Arthur's recliner because it's mine now and it feels good to be close to him

I miss him so terribly, more than I ever dreamed I would.

"Detective Peters was just here," Theodore says.

"I knew it!" Claire exclaims. "Did he come to talk to Mama?"

"He gave me this." Theodore handed the document to Claire. She reads it and looks up. "This is a search warrant."

I pull the knob and erect the recliner.

"What was he searching?" I ask Theodore.

"The house. For clues, I presume," he replies.

Claire bites her lip and shakes her head.

"Did he find anything criminally useful?" I'm sarcastic.

"I don't know. Four cops were here for an hour. They went all over the house and checked out the shed where Arthur keeps his farm implements." He looks to Claire for moral support.

Double D-D! I think to myself. *What kind of clues?*

"Come outside with me, Claire," Theodore tells her and I know whatever he has to say is not for my ears. I'm so tired I go into my bedroom, drop my big purse on the chair and lie down in my bed. . .

A Week ago, on Friday

"Hey, Lorene, glad you made it here to play cards," I say.

The four of us are seated around the square table at the Senior Citizen Center. We're about to play Canasta for three hours.

Lizzy Hinson sits to my right, and Jane Murphy is on my left. Lorene sits directly across from me. We are delighted to be together.

"Did you see in the church bulletin where Percy Ives died?"

"No, Lizzy, what did he die from?" I deal out the cards.

"Stroked out right in front of Cynthia. She almost croaked."

"That's terrible," Lorene says. "When is Percy's funeral?"

"It hasn't been set yet. He's been embalmed and stored in a cooler for a while," Lizzy says. "He's probably got relatives that live far away who want to attend his funeral. It's about the only time families all get together." She studies her Canasta hand.

I chuckle to myself. "So true. Someone has to die before we have a family reunion. Seems people would rather see their relatives dead than to visit them when they're alive. It's really a shameful crime."

"Talk about crime," Lorene says from across the table. "Did Arthur bring in that nasty muddy red clay on his boots into your kitchen yesterday like my Crawford did?" She glares at me.

I lock eyes with Lorene. "Arthur was wearing his boots and he ruined my new rug at the backdoor," I tell her.

"My beige carpet in the den still has red stains," she complains.

We look at each other and grin. "Two dead on Crystal Creek!"

The four of us laugh. But I know we love our husbands. . .

I suddenly bolt from my catnap. It's only a dream, a playback of what I said that I shouldn't have said to anyone. And now that Lorene's Crawford and my Arthur were found dead on the same day, it looks bad for us. Is that why Detective Peters was here?

"Mama?" Claire calls from the doorway. "Lunch is ready."

"Okay, I'll be there in a minute." I tinkle in the hall bathroom and drag my tired old body across the den and into the kitchen.

"What's for lunch?"

"Deli turkey sandwiches," Claire replies. "I cut up some fresh fruit since Ted is on a diet." She hands him half a sandwich with a bowl of fruit, then sits down at the table to enjoy her food.

Ask me, Theodore cheats. How long has he been on that diet? Five years or more, it seems. Claire feeds him healthy meals at home, but I suspect he goes out with the boys and gets pizza or hamburgers with french-fries. But my daughter has a perfect figure, always has.

Theodore says a nice blessing over our food.

Claire joined the First Baptist Church in Nashville right after she married Theodore thirty-two years ago. Being raised with church values, she rarely drinks alcohol but he does when he's out with the boys, every chance he gets. I wonder if their marriage will last.

But they still seem to be in love.

"Dorothy, we need to talk about something Claire told me."

I look hard at my daughter. "What did you tell Theodore?"

"I told him you told me that you said something to someone you should not have said, and that you refused to tell me what it is."

I scratch my head. I'm not going to tell her what Lorene and I said last Friday when we were playing cards at the Senior Citizen Center. It doesn't look good, considering . . .

"Dorothy."

Theodore says my name so seriously I worry a bit.

"You may be in trouble," he says.

"Why? I didn't kill Arthur. Is that what Butch thinks?"

"Mama!"

I don't' like the way Claire says my name.

"There must be a good reason why Detective Peters searched your house," he says. "Why don't you tell me what you said and where you said it, and to whom you said it. I might can help."

I inhale deeply. "Nobody can help. Arthur is dead!"

I get up from the table and go out the backdoor.

I'm double D-Ding and S-Sing to myself with every step I take.

Why in the world did Lorene and I say, "Two Dead on Crystal Creek?" It will surely not work in our favor, especially now that we are both beneficiaries to huge life-insurance policies.

Does Butch think we're so stupid we'd say something like that on Friday and murder our husbands on Monday?

Is he nuts? Or does he hate me that much?

A Time to Investigate

7

Sunday, October 31ˢᵗ

SUNDAY ROLLS AROUND AND I don't feel like going to church. I have not missed attending since I had a nasty kind of influenza two seasons ago. I go to Sunday School but Arthur usually joins me for the ten o'clock service. It never takes Brother Kenny more than ten minutes to put Arthur in a stupor. I worry he didn't make it all the way to Heaven. Catholics pray for their dead loved ones.

Why can't Methodists? Is God prejudiced against us?

It's storming outdoors this morning as I look out my bedroom window. I grope in the darkness to find my wristwatch, then realize I've misplaced it, or it simply fell off my wrist from a broken clasp.

I tiptoe into the den, switch on the overhead light, and squint at the wall clock. It's 6:30 a.m. Out the den window I spy bitter dark clouds draping from the sky like monsters of various shapes and shades of black. I don't expect to see the sun shine anytime soon.

I drag my sluggish body into the kitchen, every step I take my bones suffer from Old Arthur. I'm alone. Claire isn't up yet.

I fill the coffee pot with tap water and measure out the right amount of ground Columbian beans to put in the filter cup. That done, I sit down at the breakfast table and wait for the coffee to drip while trying to make sense out of yesterday. A few minutes later, the coffee bubbles into the glass pot as the coffeemaker hisses the job is done.

"Mama?"

I look up and Claire is standing there.

"I didn't mean to wake you, honey," I apologize as the rain drums hard on my roof. "Coffee's ready, I expect you need a cup."

"You didn't wake me, I set the alarm on my iPhone."

Claire walks over to the counter, fills two mugs with coffee, then adds ample cream to both. Back at the table, she hands me my mug.

"Thank you." I gratefully take a swig.

"Mama, we got a call from the kids last night," Claire says.

"Is somebody sick?" She refers to my grandchildren.

"No, but Ted and I need to go home this morning and take care of some things," she says to me as she drinks more coffee.

I say nothing, so she says, "Will you be okay alone?"

Alone. There's that blasted word again. *I am alone.* Nothing in the world now is going to change that. "Sure, go home, Claire."

"I'll be back first thing tomorrow morning," she assures me.

"No hurry, I'll be fine."

"On my way into Nashville, I'll stop at Kroger and grab some microwave dinners for Ted to nuke next week. He doesn't like to cook like Daddy did." I see the sadness in Claire's eyes.

"Your daddy loved fixing breakfast." I hold her hand. "He made the best country ham and biscuits you'd ever want."

Then wonder if I can ever look at a piece of ham again.

"Good morning!" Theodore appears, all chipper and dressed in casual clothes for the dreary day. "I'm taking my wife out for breakfast." He prances over to the coffeemaker for a cup of Joe.

"Oh?" I look at Claire. "Is today a special occasion?"

"It's our anniversary," Theodore says and I feel like a heel. How can I forget my daughter's anniversary? It's Halloween.

I look at Claire first then Theodore. "I didn't get you a gift, I'm so, so sorry." I lay my head on the table and resist bawling.

Then magically my daughter's hand clamps one shoulder while Theodore squeezes the other. "It's okay, Mama, we understand you have a lot on your plate." His words comfort me tremendously.

I look up at Theodore and say, "I love you, Ted."

This is the first time I've called him Ted and he's called me Mama since he married Claire decades ago.

"We both love you," Claire adds then bends down to hug me.

I sit up, dry my eyes on my housecoat then stand up.

"You two love birds, go on. Enjoy the day. Have a great breakfast and do whatever needs doing at your house. If I get lonely, I'll call one of my girlfriends to come over and keep me company."

"Okay then," Claire looks at Ted, "we should get going soon."

43

While they dress and make preparation to leave for Nashville, I fix myself a bowl of Raisin Bran Cereal from Aldi's. I shop there sometimes because some items are cheaper than Walmart or Kroger.

"We're leaving now," Claire calls out from the backdoor. "Call my cellphone if you need anything. I'll tell the kids you said hello."

"You do that, Claire." To Ted, I say, "Thanks for taking such good care of my daughter. Happy anniversary!"

As they drive away, I realize something new has already come into my life since Arthur left me. Theodore calls me Mama and I call him Ted. It gives me a warm and fuzzy feeling that I have the support of my family. I need to find a way to weather through a memorial service for Arthur. After that, I will have to figure out if I can live alone in this big old house. But I won't think about that yet.

The sun peeks from dingy clouds late morning and by one o'clock the yard is dry enough to rake fallen leaves. A light breeze stirs as the sun heats the temperature into the high sixties.

I go outside and look up. As the sunshine warms my face, I pray that God is not too offended that I've missed church and will do work on His day of rest. But I can't just sit around the house alone and think terrible thoughts. It would be far too depressing.

After I've bagged the dead leaves in large plastic garbage bags, just like Arthur always did, I go back in the house and fix myself a tall glass of cold sweet tea. Then I decide I want to see where Arthur died. I use the landline to call Clyde Willems.

"Clyde, this is Dorothy Powell."

"Mrs. Powell, how are you?" he speaks respectfully.

"Clyde, if you're not terribly busy, I want to see the place by the creek where Arthur died. Will you take me there?"

"Now?"

"Yes, if you're not too busy."

"I can be at your house in about fifteen minutes."

"Thank you." I end the call, feeling proud of my bravery.

Clyde lives two and a half miles down the gravel road behind our house in his daddy's old log cabin. He's been a resident of Maury County for fifteen years. He was married twice but single now.

44

I wonder why Clyde is divorced. He seems so nice. In some ways, he is Arthur's best friend. *Was*, I remind myself.

I trade my slippers for a sturdy pair of rubber rain shoes then sit at the breakfast table to wait. I hear Clyde's blue pickup truck trudging up the gravel driveway to my house. Before he honks his horn for me, I'm outside and locking the backdoor. Stepping into the mushy yard, I climb in his truck on the passenger side.

"Thanks, Clyde, for doing this," I tell him.

"No problem, Arthur was a good friend."

The truck seats are surprisingly clean, covered with a cotton print pattern. "Nice afternoon for a stroll," he comments.

Clyde puts the truck in reverse and backs up until he can turn around in the circular drive out front of my house. We drive down the gravel driveway and turn left on Crystal Creek Road. Harvest time is over but we pass fields of bailed hay not yet gathered.

The same creek that flows through our property cuts a drunken path through Crawford and Lorene Perkin's property.

"Clyde?"

"Yes, Ms. Powell?"

"Please call me Dorothy. You were a friend of Arthur's so now you're my friend." I smile, hoping he doesn't get the wrong idea.

"We'll have to turn up a dirt road, uh, Dorothy," he says. "Then we walk or ride my four-wheeler the rest of the way to the creek."

"I'll walk, if it's not too far." I cannot imagine myself climbing on the ATV with Clyde, holding onto him like he was my savior—which he would be if he kept me from falling off the blame thing.

"How far is the walk, Clyde?"

"'Bout a half mile walk," he answers.

I hold up a bottle of water. "I'll be fine if we take it slow."

Until this week, I've been going to the Health Club in town to join a women's senior swim class twice a week. For an eighty-year-old woman, I'm not in the worst of shapes. Except for arthritis.

By the time we walk to the creek I'm huffing and puffing. But I dare not let any wolf blow down my house—which is my old body.

"I found him right there." Clyde points to the sandy soil riddled with small pee gravel. *Oh, Lordy!* I can almost see Arthur's print in the sand, but I know by now the rain has washed it away.

"Where was his tractor?" I inquire.

"Over there." Clyde points. "About ten feet away."

I puzzle over his answer. "Then how did Arthur fall off and where is the big rock that hit him on the head?" I start to understand why Butch thinks my husband's death is not natural.

"It's too far away for Arthur to fall off," I conclude.

"I think so, too," Clyde says, a frown on his tan wrinkled face.

"Does Arthur have any enemies?" I ask.

Clyde shakes his head. "Ever 'body loved him."

I think that, too. If I were Detective Butch, I might think Arthur's wife did the killing for the big life-insurance payoff.

We stand a moment in the brisk warm breeze.

"Do you want to go home now?" Clyde asks.

"No," I say. "Do you know where Crawford Perkins died?"

"We can talk to Lorene and ask her," he says.

"Let's go back to my house and I'll phone her first."

At the house, I invite Clyde inside and fix him a glass of cold sweet tea to drink while I phone Lorene. He watches and waits.

"She says to come on over," I report.

Clyde rides with me in my Cadillac over to the Perkins' house. The car windows are down and a breeze blows across our faces. I think this must be one of those rare moments in life when a person really feels alive. I relish the thought as long as possible.

Lorene lives three miles down the main highway.

She stands on the front porch as I drive up the long gravel road to her brick home. I park my Cadillac close to the porch and switch off the engine. Clyde gets out first as Lorene approaches.

"I called my son Sam and he's coming over to show you where Crawford's body was found," Lorene says right off the bat.

"They're going to cremate my Arthur," I tell her.

"Sam thinks we should do the same for Crawford."

"Did they autopsy him?"

Lorene nods, tears in her eyes. "A heart attack."

"When will Sam be here?" I ask.

"That's him driving up now." Lorene points to a shiny red Camry. "Sam's a firefighter now, did I tell you that?"

"He also works at the post office, too. Right?"

As soon as Sam parks his car behind mine, I go over to greet him. "Thanks for coming and helping me out," I tell him.

"No problem, you and Mama are good friends," he says with an all-American smile. Sam is tall, lean and muscular. Quite handsome.

"The creek runs through the property a mile behind the house. We'll have to drive Daddy's old truck down the dirt road and walk the rest of the way." He walks around the side of the house.

"Are you coming, Lorene?" I inquire.

She shakes her head no. I understand it's too hard for her. It's hard for me, too, but now that I know Arthur's death is not an accident, I have to see the other crime scene, too.

Oh, Lordy! I'm sounding just like Detective Butch.

A Time to Question

8

CLYDE, SAM, AND I stand on the sandy bank of Crystal Creek a mile behind Lorene's house. The land belongs to her now that Crawford is dead. "I don't understand why both Arthur and Crawford died where they did," I say to Sam. "Did your father have any enemies?"

"No, Ms. Powell, he was loved by many in this community."

I nod my head. "Clyde said the same about Arthur. I wonder if gambling had anything to do with their deaths." I ponder the idea.

"What do you mean?" Clyde is disgruntled over my suggestion.

"Daddy looked forward to his Poker games two Friday nights a month," Sam offers. "I don't think any of his card buddies would hurt him or Arthur." They stand there, pondering over death.

"I've seen enough," I say. "Let's go back and talk to Lorene."

"Yes, ma'am," Sam respectfully says but Clyde remains quiet.

We walk half a mile, climb in Crawford's work truck, and Sam drives us back to the house. "It's a nice afternoon," I comment.

"Yes, it is," Sam agrees. "Rare for late October."

Clyde still doesn't have anything to say. He's in a funk.

Lorene has made coffee to go with her orange-slice cake. The guys sit on the back porch eating their ample slices while Lorene and I are in the kitchen. "Did you see where Crawford died?"

"Yes, I did, Lorene. Same as for Arthur."

"Don't you think that's odd?" She sips her coffee.

I heave a sigh. "I'm in trouble, Lorene."

She sets her cup on the counter and glares at me. "Why?"

"I think Detective Peters believes I had something to do with Arthur's death to get the half-million-dollar insurance money."

Lorene appears horrified. "Well, if you're in trouble, so am I."

"Do you think Lizzy Hinson told Butch what we said when we last played cards with the girls?" I'm referring to Detective Peters.

"I wouldn't be surprised," Lorene grumbles. "It's not the first time we've said something like that in public. In fact, we've said it dozens of times. I'm going to kill so-and-so if he does so-and-so again." She glares at me. "My mama did the same thing."

"But we didn't literally mean it." I defend both of us.

"No, but we still said it and people heard it."

"Words have meaning." I nod. "Words have power."

She nods as the guys come back into the kitchen.

"I need to get back to my truck, Dorothy," Clyde says. "I have some errands I need to run this afternoon." He's sweating profusely.

Lorene is surprised Clyde calls me by my first name.

"Thanks for your hospitality, Lorene, we'll go now."

She hugs me. "Keep me posted on anything new."

"I will—oh, I saw you put out a sign at the end of your road."

"Yeah, I don't want no trick-or-treaters showing up at my door tonight," she says and I'm reminded that I usually have adults with children stop by my house to say hello and collect candy treats.

"Let's go, Clyde. I need to run to Dollar General and load up on candy for tonight." He's anxious to leave, and I wonder why.

Back at my house, I watch Arthur's field hand drive away and wonder what he knows about Arthur's death that he's not telling me.

Or maybe anyone.

What big secret is Clyde hoarding? If I knew, would it put me in a better light? That is something I will ponder on for a while.

Darkness descends on the countryside around five p.m. I have a big plastic bowl full of suckers and soft candies sitting by the front door that I'll dole out to trick-or-treaters who knock on my door.

I surrender, no tricks tonight, please!

The doorbell buzzes around six. I hurry to the front door and peek through a side-glass panel. It's Beverly, my closest neighbor on my left. Her two children, eight and ten, are dressed to kill.

Literally, Dracula and Satan.

I open the door and tremble.

"Ohoooo!" I act like I'm so frightened.

"Trick or treat!!" They extend their colorful Halloween buckets.

I wink at Beverly and put a handful of candies in each bucket.

"I'm so sorry about Arthur," she mouths quietly.

"Thank you," I mouth back and then they get in the car and Beverly drives away, leaving me feeling utterly alone in the subdued darkness. With glassy eyes, I glance around my front yard.

The shrubs need trimming, but I'm no hand at using an electric trimmer. There is beauty in the night as the three-quarter moon casts a mellow haze over the grassy meadow beyond the gravel road.

I thank God that Claire is coming back tomorrow to be with me.

Alone sucks. I go back inside the house, close the door, and wait in the foyer for another spook to knock on my door for treats.

A Time to Speak Up

9

Monday, November 1ˢᵗ

I WAKE UP LATE ON MONDAY because trick-or-treaters knocked on my front door until well after ten last night. Halloween was in full force with the goblins out and the werewolves baying at the moon.

I hear footsteps in the hallway by my bedroom.

It must be Claire. But what if it's a burglar?

I hop out of bed and grab Arthur's pistol from the nightstand, tiptoe over to my closed bedroom door and listen for sounds.

"Mama?" Claire taps on the door.

I open it and hide the pistol behind my back.

"You scared me."

"I'm sorry." She looks at me hard. "You never sleep late."

"You think I had a stroke and died in my sleep?" I ask.

"No, but, uh, I wasn't sure what to think."

I should be so lucky, I tell myself. *Poor Lance. Poor Arthur.*

"Have you had breakfast?" I ask her as I put on my housecoat.

"Yes, I picked up a sandwich and a cup of coffee at McDonald's on my way over," she tells me, "but I'll have a second with you."

We hug then walk through the den and into the kitchen.

"Did you have a lot of trick-or-treaters last night?" she asks

"Lordy, yes! I think their parents were curious to look me in the eye to see how I was taking Arthur's death." I notice Claire is busy at the cabinet making the coffee. "Makes me wonder if Lizzy Hinson has been gossiping about me." I commiserate over the idea.

Claire turns around, her mouth half open as if to ask me a question. Then she does. "Mama, tell me the truth. Did you say something to Elizabeth that you never should have said?"

We're back to the same ol' question. And I'm worn down.

"Yes, I did," I admit.

"What did you say, Mama?"

"Both Lorene Perkins and I said the same thing. Something not so nice, but was meant as a joke. It might've been taken the wrong way by the right people." I clamp my lips. The cat's out of the bag.

"Sit down, Mama." It's a direct order. "As soon as we've got our coffees, I want you to start from the beginning and tell me what you and Lorene said, and don't you dare leave anything out!"

I collapse in a chair at the table, feeling chastised. Claire waits for the coffee to drip then brings two mugs to the table.

"Here's your coffee, *now* I'm listening."

"You know Arthur plays Poker with Crawford Perkins every other Friday night. They have for years. There's six other men that play with them. Sometimes one of them drops out and another replaces them. Well, Lorene and I play cards once a week down at the Senior Citizen Center, too." I pause for a breath.

"What has this got to do with Daddy's death?" Claire asks.

"I'm getting to it, honey, bear with me."

She nods and I'm the star of our conversation again.

"Well, both your daddy and Crawford have a bad habit of not taking their shoes off when they come from the field—you know how much it rains in October. Well, Lorene and I don't like it a bit. We have this saying: Two Dead on Crystal Creek."

There, it's out in the open and I'm relieved.

"Mama!" Claire is horrified. "You say that in front of people?"

"No. Just friends. I'm not stupid. And we were teasing."

"What prompted you to repeat this horrible statement, and when exactly did you say this and to whom?" Claire glares at me hard.

To whom. I just can't get past my daughter's perfect English, perfect figure, perfect hair, perfect children, perfect husband, and perfect life. "Friday a week ago, when we were playing cards."

Claire offers no response.

"So, it seemed obvious to me and Lorene that Arthur and Crawford must have been together when they got red mud on the bottom of their boots. Your daddy ruined my new kitchen rug by the backdoor. And Crawford soiled Lorene's beige rug in her den."

I look at Claire. "Then we said what we always say when we hate what Arthur and Crawford did: Two Dead on Crystal Creek."

Claire bites her lips. It's not a good sign. She touches my hand.

"I know, I know . . .it doesn't look good for us now that our husbands have died on the same day by Crystal Creek, but we did not commit murder. We did not hire someone else to do it for us."

Claire's mouth is open but nothing comes out.

"Do you think we are stupid?"

"No, Mama, I don't think you're stupid. But Detective Peters doesn't care. He thinks he has a murder case and he's jumping up and down to solve it. He doesn't care who gets hurt as long as he looks good. Butch has always been an asshole. He was in high school and he still is!" She is on a roll and I'm proud of her.

And best of all, I know my daughter is on my side, regardless how this thing shakes out. I'm happy. Truly happy.

"I'll make us breakfast." Claire gets up from the table.

"I want cereal," I tell her, "and I'll fix it myself."

Claire helps me clean the house during the morning. I remove all the perishable food from my fridge that friends have brought to the house last week. What is still good, like the roast beef, I parcel out in plastic containers and freeze enough for one person.

I am alone. And I know it. And I have to convince Butch somehow that I had nothing to do with Arthur's death. Then I'll move on with my life. *What's left of it.*

Claire answers the landline late morning.

I watch her expression as it turns from normal to concerned.

"We'll be right there," she says.

I get up from Arthur's recliner, mine now, and walk into the kitchen. "Who was on the phone, Claire?"

"That was Detective Peters. He wants to see us."

"Did he say if Arthur's autopsy report was ready?"

"No, but I expect that's why he wants to talk to us," Claire replies. "I need to take a shower and change clothes. I'm all sweaty from being upstairs. You and Daddy never go up there so you don't run the system." She shakes dust from her ruby-red hair.

"I know what you're thinking. That this house is too big for me. Well, it was too big for me and Arthur decades ago, but I couldn't bring myself to sell it and he loved to putter around the farm."

"We'll talk about putting the house on the market after we bury Daddy," Claire tells me. "First, we have to find out what really happened to him." She looks at me. "We'll leave for town soon."

I shower and change clothes, too. We meet at the backdoor and go out to the shed. Claire drives my Cadillac to Columbia and we pull into the police station's parking lot. We pass Lizzy Hinson as we enter the station. Claire looks at me. "She's told Butch."

I nod. *She couldn't wait to spill her guts*, I think. *Double D-D!!*

Butch's secretary, Ellie, is in a foul mood today. She mutters a hello and resumes typing on her computer. Butch opens the door to his office and comes out. "Come on in, ladies."

I trail Claire into his office. When the door closes, I feel as if the walls have eyes and are slowly closing in on me, squeezing the life out of me. "Am I going to jail for killing Arthur?" I blurt out.

A smile trembles on Butch's lips. "Did you, Dorothy?"

"Butch!!" Claire exclaims. "You can't believe that!"

He slams the autopsy report on his desk for Claire to read.

Claire takes a moment to peruse the contents.

"I don't know what all this means," she admits to Butch.

"Arthur did not fall off his tractor and hit his head. He was struck on the back of the head with a blunt object." He shows us a photograph. "Dorothy, do you recognize what this is in the picture?"

He hands the glossy photograph to me.

"Yes, it's a wrench like Arthur uses. He keeps it in the shed."

"Correct." Butch leans back in his office chair, his hands resting on his stomach, a snarly grin on his face I despise.

"What are you intimating?" Claire asks him.

"This is Arthur's implement. We found it in our search."

"Okay?" I wait to see what he's getting at.

"It has fingerprints and blood on it."

"Okay?" I wait to see what he's getting at.

"Your fingerprints and Arthur's blood."

"Impossible!" Claire exclaims as she leaps to her feet.

Butch holds out a restraining hand. "Settle down, Claire."

She drops in her chair, horrified at the implication.

"Dorothy Jean Powell, you have the right to remain silent . . ." he reads me my Miranda Rights because he's going to arrest me.

This is so unbelievable I barely hear what Butch is reading to me because my thoughts are too loud. I'm still in a fog as he buzzes the front desk and a deputy comes into the office and handcuffs me.

I look at Claire. She can't believe this is happening, either.

An eighty-year-old woman who has never gotten a parking ticket. A former school teacher. An upstanding citizen of Maury County. A good, faithful wife to Arthur. I am not a murderer.

"You can have a court-appointed attorney," Butch tells me.

"My husband is a lawyer, he'll represent Mama," Claire says.

"Is he a trial lawyer?" Detective Butch inquires.

"No."

"The charge is Murder One. You might want to rethink that, Claire," Butch says a little to curt for my liking.

"When will Mama be arraigned?" Claire asks him.

"She'll spend the night in jail and face a judge tomorrow."

"Is that necessary? Mama is, uh, not young anymore, and I don't feel that she's safe in jail. Can you guarantee her safety, Butch?"

Claire calls him that and he cringes from her lack of respect.

"Dorothy will be fine. We'll put her alone in a cell."

Alone. There goes that word again. I hate it.

* * *

Claire goes through every room of her parent's house. If there is anything Mama missed that would clear her name, she wants to find it. Her cell phone rings. It's Ted calling back.

"What's up, Claire? I'm kind 'a busy here."

"Mama has been arrested for Murder One."

Ted curses. He seldom curses.

"I know, it seems impossible. I thought you might represent her at the hearing tomorrow when she's arraigned in court," Claire says.

"I'm not a trial lawyer, Claire."

55

"I know, Detective Peters said the same thing. He thinks I should hire a lawyer with court experience. Do you know anyone in Maury County I can contact and discuss Mama's predicament?"

Claire nervously waits for information.

"I'll get back to you with a name. I really need to go now."

"Okay, Ted. Please pray for Mama."

"Will do."

Claire punches END on her cell and walks into the master bedroom. She wonders if Mama went through Daddy's pants pockets looking for anything unusual. She removes his clothes from the closet racks and tosses them on the bed. The dress pants, his shirts, jeans, overalls, suits, and coats. Seeing them all at once is overwhelming and tears start to drizzle down her cheeks.

"Oh, Daddy, what am I going to do with all of your clothes?"

Claire considers calling the Help Center to come and get them.

"Okay, Daddy. Give me something that will help Mama."

She spends the next hour going through every pants and coat pockets and finds nothing. Then she searches the dresser drawers.

His billfold is lying in the right lower drawer.

"Okay, Daddy, let's see what you're hiding in here."

It feels good to speak aloud to herself. Helps with progress and lends some comfort. She removes his two credit cards, his driver's license, Social Security and insurance cards, from his billfold and lays them on the king bed to view. Then she searches the billfold's tight pockets. Her finger snags a piece of paper with writing on it.

I owe you $10,000 dollars.

The note is handwritten and signed by Clyde Willems.

"What in the world?" *Is this a motive for murder?*

It will certainly put doubt in the judge's mind that somebody other than Mama had a reason to end Daddy's life. Things like this do not happen to decent law-abiding families. Then Claire wonders about Crawford Perkins, her daddy's good friend, the one that went somewhere with him and got red mud on the soles of his boots.

Did someone take Crawford's life because he knew about the I.O.U. promissory note? She would certainly talk to Butch about it.

A Right Time for Sharing

10

"MS. PERKINS, THIS IS Claire Burkes. I'd like to come over and talk to you if it's a convenient time. I have some information that will surely interest you." She waits for a response.

"About my Crawford?"

"That's what I need to find out," Claire says.

"Okay, come on. Have you had lunch?"

"No," Claire says, realizing food was the last thing on her mind.

"Then I'll make us a sandwich. It's after two and I'm hungry."

"I'll be over in fifteen minutes."

Claire removes the Cadillac keys from her purse and goes out to the shed. She notices that the car needs a gas fill up. She'll do that the next time she's in town. Why does Clyde Willems owe Daddy ten thousand dollars? And why hasn't he said anything about it?

Is he ashamed or hiding something sinister?

"Well, Daddy, trust me, I'm going to find out."

Lorene is standing on the porch as Claire drives up and parks.

"What's this about, Claire?" Lorene asks from her perch.

Claire pushes out a breath she's been holding, gets out of the car and walks up the steps to the porch landing. They gaze at one another.

"Has something else bad happened?" Lorene inquires.

"Yes, Ms. Perkins. Mama's been arrested, accused of murdering my daddy." Claire hitches a breath. "I thought you should know."

"What?" Lorene's eyes widen with disbelief.

"Detective Peters found evidence that Mama handled the murder weapon used to strike Daddy's head. He found the wrench in the work shed with Daddy's blood and Mama's fingerprints on it."

"My Lord!"

As Lorene staggers, Claire thinks she might fall.

"Let's go inside so you can sit down, Ms. Perkins."

At Lorene's insistence, they first have lunch.

"Now, tell me all of it," Lorene says as they sit in the sun parlor.

"This morning I found a piece of paper tucked in the pocket of Daddy's billfold," Claire tells Lorene. "It was a promissory note. Clyde Willems signed it. He owes Daddy $10,000."

Lorene is surprised. "Whatever for?"

"Since Crawford died the same day as Daddy, is it possible he knew about the I.O.U.?" Claire asks.

"Well, sure, it's possible."

"I'm thinking that maybe their deaths are connected."

"So, you're saying my Crawford was murdered by the same person that killed your daddy?" She tries to wrap her mind around so sinister a thought. "My husband had a heart attack."

"Maybe someone scared him to death," Claire concludes.

"Have you told Detective Peters about finding the note?"

"No, I wanted to talk to you first," Claire replies. "Will you look through your husband's things for anything useful?"

"That relates to the note you found," Lorene clarifies.

"Yes," Claire says. "I'm taking this note to town and showing it to Detective Peters. I want him to know Clyde has as much a reason to kill my daddy as it appears my mother does. By that time, I'll have the name of a good trial attorney to represent Mama."

Claire gets up and grabs her purse.

"I'm going now, I'll call you later today."

"Okay, dear." Lorene walks Claire to the door. "Be safe."

* * *

As Claire pulls into the police parking lot, she thinks of what Lorene said. *Be safe.* Then wonders if this knowledge also puts her life in danger. She gets out of the car, locks up, and goes inside the station. Ellie is laughing. She's in a much better mood today.

"I need to speak to Detective Peters," Claire says.

"He's at lunch."

"Where?"

"You can wait for him here." Ellie points to a chair.

Claire doesn't want to wait, but what choice does she have?

Butch is back at the station in forty-five minutes. He walks like a cock about to crow and wake the morning. It's almost four p.m.

"Your mama is just fine, I called Jake at the jail to check."

"Thank you," Claire says. "Can we talk privately a minute?"

He checks the time on his phone.

"I have fifteen, come in my office."

When the door is closed, Claire says, "I found this note in Daddy's billfold." She hands it to Butch.

He reads it and blinks. "This may change everything."

"I hope so, I know Mama loved my daddy. She wouldn't kill him or ask someone else to do it for her. Will you talk to Clyde Willems about the note?" She doesn't think the field hand is capable of murder, but the note does point in another direction.

"Count on it. Did you hire a lawyer yet?"

"No, my husband is working on getting me the name of a trial lawyer in Maury County. I hope to hire one before Mama is arraigned sometime tomorrow." She glares at Butch.

"I don't know a time yet, I'll phone you."

* * *

Dorothy sits in the jail cell on the twin bed with little padding. It is uncomfortable and hurts her tailbone. "Oh, Arthur, if you can hear me up in Heaven—if you're there close to Jesus—tell him I really need his help. She despondently stands up and stretches.

A Time for Revelation

11

Tuesday, November 2nd

THERE'S MORE TO THIS murder story than meets the eye. Lloyd has not yet informed Dorothy Powell that Clyde Willems was found dead in a drainage ditch in south Dickson County. Not likely that he murdered Arthur or Crawford Perkins, but Clyde is somehow the key to busting this case wide open. He steps out of his office.

"Ellie. Here are the names of the people I want you to contact and set up appointments with me as quickly as possible."

She stops typing and glares at him.

"Now, Ellie, if you will."

"Together or separately?" she asks.

"One at a time. Start in the morning." *Wednesday*, he thinks.

"Okay, I'll see what I can do," Ellie says, sweet on Butch.

"Are you free Friday night? Thought we might drive into Nashville and hit some of the clubs." He has an ulterior motive.

"Sure, what time can you pick me up?"

"Eight o'clock. Dress to kill."

She winks. "I can do that."

He knows she can. Ellie is a divorcee and has been flirting with him for months. She's hot and ready, and who knows, he might get lucky in love Friday night as well as pick up a lead that will tell him something new. But for now, he must concentrate on work.

* * *

Court is in session at two p.m. Tuesday. Judge James Sewell is presiding. There were eight arrests in Columbia over the weekend, seven of them minor offenses. One was a murder. An old woman coldcocked her husband for his life-insurance policy. He guesses crimes of that nature are not uncommon in America. But he knew Arthur Powell well. In fact, he played Poker with him.

This was a hearing and arraignment with no jury present.

Judge Sewell enters the Maury County courtroom through the rear door as he always does. He is sixty-eight and will retire from the bench soon. He's tired of working and has a heart condition.

James spies Detective Lloyd Peters seated at a table to his right with Assistant D.A. Daniel Farnsworth. Dorothy Powell, Arthur's wife, sits at the other table with her attorney, Melvin Pulaski.

Fairly new to Columbia, the forty-eight-year-old trial attorney moved from Nashville a couple of years back after divorcing his wife. He comes to the bench with impeccable credentials and murder trial experience. And likely costs Ms. Powell a pretty penny.

"All Rise," the bailiff calls out and the judge says, "Be seated."

During the morning session, James has ruled on the other seven cases on today's docket. He decided to hear Mrs. Powell's case after lunch. From what he's read in the newspapers, this is an intriguing case. He nods at the bailiff to begin the session.

"Case # 254," the bailiff tells Judge Sewell. "Dorothy Judith Powell is accused of Murder One." He sits down at a small table.

The judge looks at me, the defendant.

"How do you plead, Ms. Powell?"

I shakily stand up. "Not guilty, Your Honor."

"Please enter the plea into record," he tells the stenographer.

Claire notices that two reporters have slipped in the back of the courtroom to hear her mother's case. Judge Sewell notices, too. He expects an article about the widow will appear in the Nashville paper by tomorrow morning. Nothing like a murder to attract attention.

Judge Sewell clears his throat.

"Assistant District Attorney, Daniel Farnsworth, please present your case against Ms. Powell." He sits down on a stool behind the lector. He's too old to stand five days a week during sessions.

I look at the judge and wonder what he thinks of me. He played cards with Arthur every other Friday evening. When he wasn't there, Jimmy James, a local barber, filled in for him. Claire told me about Clyde's I.O.U. she found in Arthur's billfold. Will that be revealed?

Farnsworth presents the evidence into the court record and recommends the defendant pay bail and remain at home on House

Arrest due to age. I'm surprised and grateful. I realize getting special treatment in court is perhaps the only good reason for getting old.

Claire and Ted are present and they breathe more evenly at hearing the ADA's recommendation. If money is the motive for murder, Clyde's I.O.U. shines a new light on the mystery.

"Ten-thousand dollars bail and House Arrest until a time the defendant shall be heard before a jury of her peers," Judge Sewell declares with the rap of his gavel then leaves the courtroom.

"All Rise!" the bailiff calls out too late.

Claire rushes to the front to see her mother.

"Oh, Mama, I get to take you home. I was so scared."

I say, "God is good and He always makes a way."

"Let's get the jewel put on your ankle and get out of here," Claire tells me. "Those two men at the back of the courtroom are Nashville reporters." She stares at them like they're vultures.

"Do they want to interview me?" I ask. "I should tell them my side of the story. I don't want people to think badly of me."

"No, Mama. That's a terrible idea. They'll twist your words."

A policeman comes to my table and locks a metal bracelet around my left ankle. Attorney Pulaski explains to me and Claire how it works. If I venture more than fifty feet in any direction from my house, it will squeal and the police will come and get me. The bracelet has not yet been activated so Claire can drive me home.

Detective Peters will follow us and activate the device.

Where would I run if I wanted to? I'd rather be in my own house than any place in the world. This is a no-brainer.

Claire and I take the elevator down to the main floor of the historic 18th-century courthouse that sits in the middle of Columbia's business square. We go outside and the fresh air is rewarding.

I've been shut up in a compact jail cell for a day and a half. Freedom is everything. I know why the Revolutionary War was fought and blood was spilt. I am part of all that history.

Ted is out front in his Mercedes Benz with the motor running.

Claire shields me from phone flashes as we get in his car. Me, in the front seat, her in the back. He takes off like the Roadrunner.

I don't care. *Freedom is everything!*

"You doing all right, Mama?" Ted glances over at me as I tighten my seatbelt for a fast ride back to my house.

I love that Theodore calls me Mama.

"Why, Ted, I'm just peachy."

Claire snickers from the back.

It reminds me of a vacation Arthur and I took with the children to New Mexico almost too many years ago to count. Lance was ten years old and Claire was six. They constantly bickered over almost anything. Snickering and slapping at one another, Lance fussed that Claire was on his side of the car seat. It drove me and Arthur nuts.

Oh, to recover time. Good times, that is.

"Mama?"

I half turn in my seat to hear by daughter better.

"Yes, dear."

"Ted will drop us off at your house. He has to go back to work, but I plan to stay with you for the rest of this week. But I'm going home this weekend. I need to take care of our house affairs."

"I understand, dear. But you don't have to stay with me all week. Lorene can come over." We can sort out this murder mess.

"Mama, Crawford's funeral was this morning and Lorene's going to Kentucky to stay with her daughter for a while."

I don't understand why Lorene didn't tell me. I turn around and stretch my neck to see my daughter clearly.

"She can't do that to me!"

"Mama, it's already done."

"But I need her help to solve Arthur's murder!"

"Mama, that's not your job. Butch will. He's trying his best."

What does anyone know about *best*? If it were their butt going to jail for murder, I bet they wouldn't sit like a frog on a knotty log and do nothing. Gratefully, Ted doesn't drive as fast as Claire.

When we arrive home, I go inside first and spy several new dishes on the kitchen counter that friends delivered earlier this morning. I'll never eat all this food. "Claire," I call out to her.

"What is it, Mama?"

"Will you call Brother Kenny at the Methodist Church and tell him to tell my church friends not to send over any more food?"

"Sure, but you might hurt somebody's feelings," she cautions.

"They'll just have to live with the rejection."

I didn't eat the jail food served me so I was hungry. I see a large pie dish covered with aluminum foil. It's so mysterious, I uncover it.

Pecan, my favorite.

"Claire!" I call out. "Would you and Ted like a slice of pecan pie with vanilla ice cream?" I cut a big slice for myself.

Maybe it's premature to tell my church friends not to bring me food. I won't ever have to cook again if they keep feeling sorry for me. "Claire!" I call out again because she hasn't answered me.

"Sorry, Mama, I was helping Ted put my suitcase and makeup bag in the guest bedroom. What were you saying?"

She spies the pie. "Is that Lizzy Hinson's pecan pie?"

"Yes, it is. I guess she's sorry she ratted me out about . . . you know." I'm eating too fast and will likely upchuck if I don't slow down, but I'm literally starving after serving jailtime.

"You should call Elizabeth and thank her. You have no idea if she ratted on you," Claire points out. "She may have given Butch a character reference." She cuts a piece of pie for herself.

I laugh and shake my head. "Oh, the innocence of youth."

Ted comes into the kitchen to save the day.

"I'm off now, girls."

Claire kisses him on the mouth. "I'll miss you."

"Do you want to take a slice of pecan pie with you?" I ask him.

"Mama, Ted's on a diet," Claire answers for him.

Oh, the innocence of the young!

"There's plenty of frozen dishes in the freezer for you to thaw out, Ted. Be safe driving home and call me every night."

"Absolutely." Ted looks at me. "You take care, Mama."

I smile fondly at Theodore. I love that he calls me Mama.

A Time for Work

12

Wednesday, November 3rd

IT'S ALREADY NOON AND Lloyd has interviewed five of Arthur Powell's poker buddies. Judge Sewell occasionally substituted on a Friday evening, but he sat on the bench during Dorothy's hearing.

Lloyd wasn't going to query him about the murder.

Arthur was well-liked and the players spoke well of his character. They had nothing negative to say about him or Crawford Perkins. All seemed shocked to learn that Clyde Willems was found dead in a ditch in south Dickson County and wanted to know if his death was related to Arthur's and Crawford's. Lloyd wonders the same thing as he sits at his desk pondering how to proceed. His cell phone rings.

"Yeah?" he answers.

"Is this Detective Lloyd Peters?"

"Yes, it is. Who wants to know?"

"I'm Clyde Willems' half-sister, Lorita."

"How can I help you, Lorita?"

"I know what happened to Clyde," she says.

"How did you find out he died?"

"I read about it in the Dickson Herald this morning."

Lloyd curses to himself. Some cop blabbed his mouth.

"I have some information about Clyde that will interest you."

"Great! When can we get together?" Lloyd asks.

"Is there a reward for information regarding the ongoing murder investigation into the death of Arthur Powell?" she inquires.

"Is this a shakedown, Lorita? If it is, I'm not buying."

"No, sir. This is real info."

There's silence at the other end of the line.

"Can you come to my place in Dickson later today?"

"What time?" Lloyd hopes this is not wasted energy.

"I work as a waitress at the Cracker Barrel and I'm finished at five. I live in an apartment ten minutes away."

Lorita gives him her apartment address.

Lloyd writes it down and will meet with Clyde's half-sister at six p.m. He ends the call and wonders what new info he'll uncover.

* * *

Claire is up earlier than her mother on Wednesday. Sleeping later than usual might indicate some depression now that her daddy has been dead for going on ten days. She sits at the breakfast table catching up on her email. College friends she's kept in contact with over the decades have written condolences from all over the U.S.

People have been so kind. And she appreciates their concern.

"Claire?"

She looks up. "Mama, you slept in late again."

"Is that a problem?" I drag my weary body into the kitchen and remove a mug from the cabinet. Never mind the cream, I want my caffeine straight up this morning. I seriously need to wake up.

"Are you sick, Mama?" Claire worries.

"No, I had trouble falling asleep with this darn bracelet on my ankle. Just couldn't get comfortable in bed, so I took an *Alprazolam*."

"You took a nerve tablet?" Claire is surprised. "Aren't those habit forming?" She wonders if she should call Doctor Hammons.

"Remember, my doctor prescribed them when Lance died?"

"Mama, that was a long time ago. It's old med. Throw it away."

I walk over to the table with my cup of Joe and sit down.

"Did you find anything interesting on the internet?" I inquire.

"Some friends have emailed their condolences," Claire answers. "Which reminds me, we need to plan Daddy's memorial service."

I look at my daughter. "I'm not ready for that yet."

Claire wonders if her mother will ever be ready.

"I got a text from the funeral home last night. Daddy's body has been released from the morgue and cremated," Claire reveals.

"He's dust?" I don't know why I'm so shocked.

Poor Arthur.

"What am I going to do with his ashes, Claire?" I don't give her time to answer. "Should I put him on the fireplace mantel so I can talk to him every morning? Or scatter him on the cow pasture where he spent so much time. What would Arthur want?"

Claire is horrified at her mother's response but refrains from commenting on the matter, but rather says, "We have time to think about all that, Mama. For now, we need to honor Daddy's long life."

I inhale and say, "Thank you, Claire. You're a dutiful daughter."

Claire shuts down her computer, stands up and stretches.

"What do you want to do today, Mama?"

It's a rhetorical question. They'll be housebound.

"I want to rake my backyard and bag the leaves," I tell my daughter. "There's something truly therapeutic about work."

I understand why Arthur liked it so much.

"Didn't you do that last week?" Claire asks.

"Yes, but more leaves have fallen." My heart is crestfallen and no one's going to rake away my sadness anytime soon.

"The grass should be dry soon since it's sunny," Claire says. "Just don't stray any farther than fifty feet from the house." She walks over to the counter and removes the meaty casserole one of the Mary-Martha Circle ladies dropped off at the house this morning.

"I'm hungry, are you?" Claire asks me.

"Well, since I missed breakfast, lunch sounds good."

"Chicken casserole okay?"

Claire is bending over backwards to please me, the jailbird bound in chains to her own house. "Whatever," I answer. "I'm going to take my shower now and put on some old clothes before I eat then go out and tend to the backyard, if that's okay with you."

"Sure. Take your time, Mama. I'll warm the spaghetti in the oven on low while you get dressed," Claire says, appearing stressed.

Back in my bedroom, I make the bed. Claire helped me change the sheets on Monday, so Arthur's pillow doesn't smell of sweat. I actually miss the old guy's odors from the great outdoors. But his side of the bed will only smell of clean sheets since I'm sleeping in the bed alone. *Alone.* Boy, am I beginning to despise that word!

A Time of Discovery

13

WEDNESDAY AFTERNOON, AT the police station, time passes fast for Lloyd. With his office door shut, he has written summaries for two unsolved burglaries and filed the folders in his metal cabinet.

He glances at the time on his phone. *5:15 p.m.*

He should head out to Dickson and locate Clyde Willems' half-sister's address. *Lorita*, he recalls and wonders if she's half Spanish.

Clyde showed no signs he had foreign blood running through his veins. Then perhaps his father had two wives, one a Caucasian, the other of Spanish descent. He speculates if Lorita is beautiful.

The drive takes forty minutes due to the volume of traffic. Folks heading home after a long workday. He passes the Cracker Barrell on Highway 46 and drives his Chevy Blazer another four miles before he turns left and locates Lorita's apartment complex.

It's a three-story red-brick building with white siding. Looks fairly new, probably built in the past decade. Dickson County is growing by leaps and bounds as new residents leave tax-burdened states and move to Tennessee and take advantage of its favorable business atmosphere. Pretty upscale for a waitress worker.

Lloyd shuts off the truck's motor, gets out, and locks the doors. The walk up two flights of stairs is good exercise. Lorita opens the door to 2-B before he gets there. She's nice looking, like he thought.

Appears to be in her mid-forties, but still has a good figure.

"Detective Peters?" she says with a winsome smile.

"Yes. Ms. . . .? he doesn't know her last name.

"It's Willems, like my older half-brother's. My mother was Henry's second wife," she explains. "I was eight years old when Clyde left home for brighter scenery, but we've stayed in contact through the years. I presume you've seen Daddy's old log cabin in Maury County." He nods, it's a conversation for another time.

"May I come inside?" Lloyd politely asks.

"Sure." Lorita steps to one side and threads her slender fingers through her short black hair. Clairol-tinted, Lloyd suspects. Her eyes are enormous and a warm coffee-brown. He immediately likes her.

Inside the apartment, he glances around the living room. It's neat, furnished well with a few French antiques, and he wonders again how she can afford to live here. Is there a second job?

Or a man in her life?

"Please sit, Detective. Can I make you a drink?"

Lloyd considers the offer. It's been a stressful day.

"Scotch, if you have any," he replies.

Lorita has extensive alcoholic choices inside a mahogany corner cabinet. Resting on the dark-stained wooden shelves are bottles of renowned wines and liquors alongside stout frosted glasses.

"You live well, Lorita," he comments.

"For a waitress, you mean." She huskily laughs. "My deceased husband had a large life-insurance policy. We never had children, so he left me too soon, but well off. I work because I like to. With only a high-school education, my choices are limited."

"What kind of work did your husband do?" Lloyd asks.

"He was associated with the Mafia."

Lloyd blinks. "Did Clyde work for the Mafia?"

"Yes, he did. That's what I wanted to tell you. I think one of their guys from Nashville murdered my brother." Lorita doesn't say half-brother, so Lloyd knows she was close to Clyde and loved him.

"I thought if you shared with me what you know regarding your cases, and I tell you what I know, it might help solve three murders."

Lloyd likes Lorita even more. She's smart, a quick-study, and open with her thoughts. Normally, he would not share the details of any case with a stranger, but herein lies the opportunity to put together the whole picture and connect the three deceased victims.

"Do you think that's possible?" Lorita sips wine from a goblet.

Lloyd considers her proposal. It seems the only way to get to the bottom of a very confusing case that likely reaches all the way to Nashville and involves some sinister Mafia network.

* * *

"The yard looks great!" Claire compliments her mother. "I see you have your sewing machine out. You haven't sewn for years."

"Well," I say, "I have to find something useful to do until Butch decides I did not off your Daddy and takes this uncomfortable ankle bracelet off of me. I want to make aprons with placemats for us."

"That's a great idea, Mama. Can I help?"

"Sure, I have some bolts of fabrics stowed in a big box in one of the bedroom closets upstairs. If you'll bring down some materials, we can get started tonight." I feel strangely optimistic.

"Okay, but first let's eat our soup. Lizzy Hinson brought it over around four p.m. while you trimmed the shrubs out front."

"I think she's sorry she ratted me out," I say.

"You should call Elizabeth," Claire says. "Clear the air."

"I'll think about it. Tomorrow, maybe."

"We can eat our soup in the den and watch the six o'clock news." Claire wonders if there'll be footage on Clyde Willems' death.

After supper, Claire walks down the hall to the foyer and climbs the stairs to the second level. For fifty years, her parents have lived in this charming 1934 farmhouse. It's a five-bedroom, three bedrooms up and two down, with formal living and dining rooms, an eat-in kitchen, a nice-sized den and two bathrooms. One up and one down.

Claire begins her search for the boxed materials stowed in one of the bedroom closets. It's stuffy upstairs with the air systems shut off.

While walking down the hall, she realizes it will take someone with a growing family to buy this house when Mama decides to sell.

Successfully locating the box her mother referenced, Claire carries an armful of bolts of materials with various patterns downstairs.

"You found them!" I chirp like a happy bird.

"Yes, and the cotton blends are good quality. I'm surprised you have so many bolts. What were you thinking when you purchased all of this material?" Claire displays the fabrics on the back of the sofa.

"Well, good intentions don't always work out," I say.

Claire does not comment.

"I bought most of this material when you left for college. Lance never wanted a college education and was driving a diesel truck by that time. I meant to—I don't recall what I meant to make."

"It's okay, Mama," Claire says. "God knew you'd need this material for a time like this." She almost sounds like a Bible prophet.

"You're right, I need to have more faith that God is in charge of my destiny. He loves your daddy and has him cuddled in His arms as we speak. I know this with all my heart, Claire. God is good."

I suddenly sob. "Isn't that something?" I laugh really hard.

* * *

It's after nine and Lloyd is driving home after visiting with Lorita Willems in her Dickson apartment. She uses her maiden name to avoid the Mafia. She's something. Classy. Smart. Brave. And a lovely hostess. They had Domino's Pizza delivery around seven so they didn't need to break for supper. For the next hour, she gave him plenty of ammunition to push these murder cases forward.

He drives slowly since he has a light buzz from the alcohol. Nothing like success to make a guy heady. He recalls the recorded conversation on Lorita's cell phone that she played back for him.

Her last phone message from Clyde.

"Lorita, I'm in real trouble. They know about the money I borrowed from two good friends. I'm going away for a while. Watch out for a man named Mark Hagen. He's dangerous and he may come around asking questions about me."

Then there's a click as Clyde ends the call.

Lloyd shakes his head. He'd hit paydirt.

But first, he has to talk to the D.A. about what he's learned from Lorita, so together they can decide whether to involve the F.B.I.

* * *

Claire's not tired though it's after ten o'clock. She finishes cutting out the matching aprons from the pretty bolt of fabric that features colorful chickens and roosters on a white background.

Meanwhile, I've cut out my last placemat, a total of sixteen to divide between us. "I think we should call it a night," I say.

"I think you're right, Mama." Claire yawns.

"I'm surprised I'm still up. I usually go to bed by nine and get up before the sun rises." I yawn, too. "But then, I didn't get up till lunchtime today." I fold the cutouts and place them on the table.

"Well, I'm heading to bed," I tell my daughter.

Claire stares at me. "What?" I am finished with this day.

"Are you going to take another *Alprazolam* tonight?"

"If I can't fall asleep, I will," I tell her.

"Please call Doctor Hammons tomorrow and get a prescription for some sleeping tablets that aren't habit-forming," Claire urges me.

"All right," I agree. "But one more isn't going to kill me."

Claire frowns. She hates that word, too.

"Well, goodnight, dear." I cut off the lights in the kitchen and proceed with my task through the den as I trail Claire. She turns left toward the guest bedroom at the other end of the hall while I enter the master bedroom. *My* master bedroom.

Arthur no longer sleeps in the bed with me.

He has a better resting place in Heaven.

A Time for Action

14

Thursday, November 4th

DETECTIVE PETERS ARRIVES at the address that houses the offices of the Chief of Police, Assistant Chief, and Captain of Investigations for Maury County. It's nearly 10 a.m. Thursday morning.

Lloyd enters the foyer and approaches the front desk where an officer sits, assigned to screening visitors. "Can I help you?"

"I'm here to speak with Captain of Investigations, Marilyn Colbert," Lloyd tells the officer. "Yes, I have an appointment." He doesn't wait to be asked. He's here to inform Captain Colbert what he's learned from Clyde Willem's half-sister, Lorita.

Lloyd signs the guest register after the cop confirms his appointment with Captain Colbert.

"Go on up, she's waiting."

It's an elevator ride up to the third floor in the concrete-block building a few blocks from historic Columbia's court square with the antiquated 18th-century Maury Courthouse smack in the middle.

"Come in, Detective." Captain Colbert motions to him.

"Thank you for making time for me, Captain Colbert."

Marilyn Colbert is in her fifties, a tough woman with a tougher job. She has a doctorate in Criminal Law from the University of Tennessee, Knoxville. Early on, she excelled during her time at the Nashville Police Academy and was later invited by the Tennessee Director of the F.B.I. to work in their undercover division. Instead, she moved to Maury County to join the police force.

And she's done a bang-up job in the last twenty-five years.

"I understand this is about a murder case you're working on," she says. "Arthur Powell's, right?" Her brown eyes fade into her dark-skinned face. He doesn't respond before she says, "Have a seat. Coffee?" He complies, then answers, "No, thanks, I'm tanked out."

It's an impressive office with many framed awards displayed on the walls behind Marilyn's well-used laminated Cherry-wood desk. She sits in a chrome chair with leather seats that both swivels and rocks, the most expensive and comfortable to be purchased.

"Tell me what you've learned, Detective."

Lloyd claims the padded straight chair in front of her desk. He's glad she's closed the door. This information is for her ears only.

"About your case . . .?"

"Late yesterday, Captain, I received a call from a woman in Dickson named Lorita Willems."

At the name, Chief Colbert's dark thick brows lift.

"Yes, she's Clyde Willems' half-sister."

The Captain leans forward in her chair, interested.

"Lorita told me over the phone she had information about Clyde that would be helpful in solving his murder. Would I drive over to Dickson and meet with her?" Still, Marilyn offers no comment.

"I agreed and met with Lorita in her apartment last night." He leaves out the part about the alcoholic drinks and Domino's Pizza, which has nothing to do with his case. "It seems that mild-mannered, farmhand Clyde has a dark secret past. He's Mafia connected and has been since he moved to Maury County to live in his daddy's cabin located two-and-a-half miles down a gravel road behind Arthur Powell's place." Lloyd pauses to let his info sink in.

Chief Colbert sits tall, alert, and begins making notes.

"Feel free to tape my remarks," he tells her. "I'll be glad to repeat what I just said then continue on." He waits.

She pulls out a small recorder and turns it on.

* * *

I slept amazingly well last night. I know it's Thursday because I've started marking off the days on a Holiday Calendar I keep in the top right drawer of my dresser. I feel good this morning. I took a nerve pill at midnight, and it worked like a charm. It's late in the morning because my bedroom is bright with sunlight.

I get out of bed, take a shower, and put on fresh clothes.

I'm anxious to get back to my sewing. I didn't realize how much I missed crafting something lasting, something I can hold that won't die on me. Our project gives me something to look forward to. A tangible product I can look at and feel, like brick-and-mortar stores for hungry shoppers. I go into the den and listen for sounds.

None.

"Claire!" I call out then notice through the window that she's out in the backyard putting up a clothesline.

I go out on the porch. "What are you doing, Claire?"

"Putting up a line. I washed clothes this morning."

"I have a Sears dryer," I call back.

She walks toward me and stops at the foot of the porch steps.

"It quit working. It overheated so I unplugged it," she says.

"Okay, you can order me a new one on-line." I am rich, so what do I care how much one costs? I'll never spend half a million dollars before I join Arthur in Heaven. Might as well enjoy the money while I can. After we bury him, I might buy a ticket on one of those big boats that tours the waterways in Europe. Arthur never wanted to travel out of the country, but I can. I face the fact I am alone now

Claire and I venture into the kitchen together.

"You got up late again," she says. "Did you take a nerve tab?"

"I did and it worked marvelously. I feel like a new person."

"Mama, please call Doctor Hammons and get a prescription for a safer sleep medication," she insists. "I'll drive to town and pick it up at Walgreen's for you. Please, Mama, do this for me."

"Okay, Claire, if it will make you feel any better, but I can tell you there's nothing like *Alprazolam* to put a tired body to sleep."

We work on our sewing project all morning. When noon arrives, we stop for lunch. I didn't eat breakfast. I'm on a new cycle, not like the old one. I intend to try new things, more exciting things.

Life is not over for me.

I do as Claire requests and phone Doc Hammons after lunch.

"Okay," Claire says mid-afternoon, "I'm heading into Columbia to get your new med and refill your blood-pressure pills. Do you want me to get anything from the grocery store?"

She puts on a jacket because it's cold outside. A light snow is forecast for tonight. "Mama?"

"Oh." I was daydreaming. "Get us some Blue Bell Ice Cream."

"I noticed we have plenty of the Walmart brand," Claire says.

"I like Blue Bell better." I'll throw out the Walmart kind when she leaves. I don't care that Blue Bell costs more, I am rich now, and the bank account belongs to me. "Have a nice trip into town."

I putter around the kitchen and plan our supper. I'm surprised when someone knocks on my front door. As I traipse down the long hall toward the front of the house, I glance into the living room on my right then the formal dining room on my left. Arthur and I seldom heat this part of the house except during Thanksgiving or Christmas when we invite friends or family over for meals.

"Coming, hold your horses!" I call out to the knocker.

I peek through the stained-glass sidelight and spy Lizzy Hinson standing on my wrap-around porch. She knocks on my door again.

Claire hasn't been gone ten minutes. I wonder if Lizzy's been watching my house and wants to talk to me alone.

I smile at my silliness and open the door.

"What do you want, Lizzy?"

"Oh, Dorothy, I owe you an apology," she says first off.

"For what?" I wave her into my impressive vaulted foyer, thinking I might hire an interior decorator to refurbish the wallpaper. I should keep everything in my historic home as original as possible.

Old sells well. Except for human beings.

"I can't stay long," Lizzy is nervous, wringing her hands.

"I'm not mad at you, Lizzy," I say. "I saw you when you came out of the police station. Did you tell Detective Peters what Lorene and I said about our husbands?" Let's get the subject out and air it.

"No, I didn't. Butch called in all the ladies that played cards with you on Fridays to ask what we thought about you."

I smile. "What do you think of me, Lizzy?"

"I'm your friend, right? We all bragged on your good character and told Butch right off that he was barking up the wrong tree if he thought you had anything to do with Arthur's death."

She looks at me. "I promise, Dorothy."

I smile, relax, and hug her.

"Thanks, Lizzy. I believe you. You're a good friend."

We're still standing in the foyer.

"I was about to make myself some hot cocoa," I tell Lizzy. "It's a bit drafty in the house with the snow front blowing in."

Lizzy looks indecisive.

"The roads are already getting slick," she informs me. "Maybe I should go home. I passed Claire in her Buick on my way over."

"She went into town to pick up some meds for me," I say.

"Well, I hope she hurries. We might get four inches of snow tonight." Lizzy rubs her wrinkled hands together. "I should go."

"I'm sorry I didn't return your calls," I apologize. "I just wasn't in the mood to talk to anyone about, you know. Did you attend this month's Mary-Martha Circle meeting?" I inquire.

"Yes, everyone was there but you."

"I hope to attend in December, when life gets back to normal."

Will it ever? I wonder.

"I hope so, too." Lizzy hugs me then is out the front door.

I watch her drive away and chide myself for thinking hard of her She gossips, sure, but that's not the worst sin in the world.

Murder is. And the thought disassembles me.

* * *

Lloyd is pleased he has a plan of action to proceed with solving three murders, which he now knows are likely related. Lorita gave him the name of the person who was a liaison between Clyde and the Mafia king working an illegal prostitution ring out of Nashville.

John Ashbury. A name that sounds respectable, but is probably an alias. Mafia folks are careful with I.D.'s

Ellie is scheduled to accompany him to Nashville tomorrow night. Lloyd considers if he's putting her life in danger if she is with him at the upscale dining lounge where Ashbury frequents. The establishment is owned by a man named Dom. No last name.

His Russian-born girlfriend, Sonja somebody, works for Dom. She recruits fresh young meat to pimp out to wealthy clientele, many of them visiting Nashville from out-of-state or some foreign country.

Lloyd knows there's plenty of upscale social events throughout the year to attract visitors, including country-music shows.

Which makes him think of Claire Burkes' attorney-husband. Theodore represents some of the most popular country-western stars in Nashville. He draws up and finalizes their legal contracts with recording companies and keeps them out of tax problems.

Should he bring Theodore in for questioning?

According to Lorita, Clyde worked Maury County for the Mafia. Lloyd was having difficulty envisioning a farmhand recruiting young women to work in prostitution for a Nashville-based Mafia group. He suspects that Clyde has contacts inside the city to get leads.

Maybe the high school? Another avenue to check out.

Lorita believes Clyde agreed to work for the Mafia to pay off huge gambling debts. Before he moved into their daddy's log cabin fifteen years ago, he lived in Las Vegas and professionally gambled.

He borrowed from the Mafia to pay off his enormous debt at the Sands Casino. But his habit kept pulling him in even deeper.

Finally, he agreed to work for them to avoid a bullet.

One never knows who is the criminal until something like death happens. With this new information, Lloyd wonders if he should cut Mrs. Powell loose. She is no longer a suspect in her husband's murder, but if he does, the Mafia might notice and pull out.

Dorothy will have to suffer through another week or so until he can get a handle on solving the case.

Another problem. Why did Clyde borrow money from Arthur Powell? Did he accumulate new debts? Maybe he was tired of working for the Mafia. If Clyde confided in Arthur regarding what he'd done for these years, it would explain why he was murdered.

An autopsy confirmed that Crawford Perkins died from a heart attack. But who to say he wasn't frightened to death by a Mafia thug?

In fact, anyone who knows anything about the prostitute ring could be in danger. Including Lorita. But she already knows that and doesn't care. She wants justice for Clyde, no matter what.

A Time for Giving

15

Friday, November 5th

LAST NIGHT, I TOOK the new sleep medication at ten p.m. and slept for eight hours. I woke up at six a.m. Friday and felt refreshed.

Dadgum! The meds work. Time to face a new day.

Claire will help me finish my sewing project this morning and plans to drive home in the middle of the afternoon.

After lunch, the landline rings.

"Want me to get it, Mama?" She's already in the kitchen.

"Sure, Claire. I'm almost through pressing your apron and eight matching placemats. You can take them home with you today and show Ted." Claire grabs the receiver and says, "Hello."

"It's Arthur's attorney, Jacob Dunwoody," she informs me.

"Yes, Mr. Dunwoody?" Claire signals for me to join her in the breakfast room. I try to hear what's being said and can't.

"Is this Little Claire?" Jacob asks. "Why, I haven't laid eyes on you in a decade. How are you and Theodore doing?"

"Fine, thank you. What's this call about, Mr. Dunwoody?

"Arthur's will," he answers.

Claire tells me, "It's about Daddy's will."

"Will you bring Dorothy to my office later today so I can read both of you Arthur's Will-and Testament? I have an opening at 4:30."

"That's not possible, Mr. Dunwoody. Mama can't leave the house right now." All the while, I'm shaking my head at Claire.

Don't tell Jacob I'm wearing a leg bracelet.

"Oh, I'm sorry, is she ill?" he asks Claire.

"No." Claire bats away my hand. "Mama's under House Arrest."

If I had a wrench, I just might hit my daughter on the head.

"Whatever for?"

"It's a long story, Mr. Dunwoody. Can you come over to the house sometime tomorrow and read us Daddy's will? My husband is a Nashville lawyer and I know he'll want to be present."

"Cynthia!" he calls out. "Can you go with me to Arthur Powell's farm tomorrow? I need to read Dorothy his Will-and-Testament."

Claire hears her lyrical response, "Of course, Jacob."

"Yes. How is eleven a.m.? Our business should not take long."

"Perfect," Claire replies, "we'll see you and Cynthia then."

I am standing two feet away from my daughter, a chip on my shoulder. Maybe, a bolder. I feel like a fifth wheel. I don't know what I feel like. Everyone is making decisions for me. *D-D!*

I look hard at Claire.

"Why did you tell Jacob I'm under House Arrest?".

"He'll know soon enough when he sees your ankle bracelet."

I don't like surprises so maybe Jacob doesn't either. Besides, I may not be emotionally equipped to hear Arthur's will. He is not yet in the ground and we're already giving his things away.

"Mama, sometime we have to hear what Daddy left you," Claire says. "We need to know if it's enough for you to live on without selling the house." She drinks from a glass of water like she's thirsty.

"Of course, it's enough," I say. "The house and land have been paid off. I can live on social security for the rest of my life. Won't I get the same amount Arthur did? The feds always paid him more."

"Yes, Mama. About the insurance policy," Claire brings it up.

"Will it be included in the reading of the will?" I inquire.

"No, a representative from the insurance company will call soon and set up an appointment to talk with you. But until the murder charge is dropped, I expect you won't see a penny of the cash."

"I'm not worried about the half-million dollars. I would take Arthur back anytime over the money. Anybody who knows me should know that. It's ridiculous I have to wear this ankle bracelet."

"I'm sorry, Mama. It just so happened the circumstance of Daddy's death involved you. I need to call Ted and see if he can spend the night here. He'll want to hear what Mr. Dunwoody says."

Claire retrieves her cell phone from her purse.

"I want a cup of decaf coffee," I tell Claire as she calls Ted. "I'll perk a whole pot if you'll join me." I hear the line is ringing.

"Dadgum!" Claire says and I know she gets his voicemail.

"Ted, change of plans. When you finish work tonight, drive out to Mama's house. We need you here in the morning for the reading of Daddy's will. I love you. Call if you plan to have supper here."

"Well, life certainly spins on a dime," I comment, realizing Claire and I need to clean the den and kitchen again before Jacob comes.

"The quote is: Turns on a Dime,'" Claire corrects me. "From the movie *Ghost* when Patrick Swasey was dead and trying to get his girlfriend's attention. Demi Moore, I believe."

"Whatever." I think of what she used to say to me.

Claire walks back into the den and looks at her pretty crisp apron that matches eight placemats. "Mama, you did a superb job."

"I used to sew a lot. Maybe I will do more now that I'm alone."

Alone. There goes that dratted word again.

* * *

Detective Lloyd Peters exits his office and walks over to face Ellie. He leans over the desk with the support of his hands.

"Can we talk alone?"

Ellie, with her big emerald eyes, looks up at her boss.

"Now?"

"My office." He turns around and retraces his steps.

Ellie puts the phone on voicemail and hurries after Butch. Once she's inside his office, he closes the door, leans close and kisses her.

"Wow! Who's gonna answer the phone?"

"This won't take long, Ellie, I need to tell you something."

He notices her expression of both anger and disappointment.

"No, I'm not breaking our date tomorrow night!"

She clamps her lips. "Then what is the big secret?"

"On the contrary, I need your help with some undercover work," he tells her. "It's dangerous. Are you up to it?"

Their eyes momentarily lock.

"If you kiss me one more time like you did before, count me in."

* * *

I'm seated in *my* recliner in the den in *my* house studying the half-dozen keys on Arthur's big metal keyring. I wonder if one of them fits a door to Clyde Willems' old cabin. "Claire!" I call out.

She hurries into the den like I've set the house on fire.

"What do you want, Mama?"

She cradles an armful of bath towels like she's holding a dozen babies. The thought makes me miss my son. *Poor Lance.*

"Will you do me a favor, dear?"

I hold out Arthur's keyring as she approaches.

She appears puzzled. "Something with Daddy's keys?"

"Will you drive your daddy's pickup truck down the gravel road and see if one of these keys' fits Clyde's cabin? I'd go, but for these."

I point to my ankle bracelet. *Double S-S!*

"Isn't that considering trespassing?" Claire asks.

"Probably, but Clyde doesn't care and I won't tell."

"What are you looking for, Mama?"

"I don't know. *Clues?* Anything that relates to Arthur's death. Maybe Clyde keeps an old-fashioned personal phone directory with the numbers of his good friends or family members."

I stare at my daughter. "I know. Butch has already looked."

"Exactly!" Claire walks into the kitchen and enters the laundry room. I'm a step behind. "Please. I have a hunch."

Claire drops the dirty towels in the laundry basket and faces me. "A *hunch*, huh?"

"I'll make a cherry pie for our supper if you'll do it for me."

Claire hugs me. "Of course, I will. But you don't have to bake."

"I want to. I'm hungry and Ted loves my cherry pie."

"Okay, put on the wash for me and I'll go do it now."

I walk Claire out on the porch. There's a light powder of snow coating the landscape from Sunday night's snow, but sunlight has melted the roadways. I watch Claire drive away in Arthur's truck and envision him behind the wheel headed off to the hayfield.

I miss my husband. *If he were only here . . .*

Claire drives down the gravel road for two-and-a-half miles and spies the old log cabin up ahead. There's a dark-blue Honda parked out front and she wonders if it belongs to one of Clyde's relatives.

She parks the truck, gets out and taps on the front door.

A beautiful young woman with short inky-black hair and lovely blue eyes that sparkle like crystals opens the door.

"Who are you?" she asks.

"A neighbor," Claire replies. "Who are you?"

"Clyde's granddaughter," she replies. "What do you want?"

The young woman with a foreign accent is rude. Maybe it would be better if she apologizes and leaves the woman to her task.

"I'm Arthur Powell's daughter, Claire. I came to see if Daddy left anything in your grandfather's cabin. Clyde was his field hand."

"The elderly man that died by the creek bed," Sonja recalls.

"Yes, may I come in? I won't be long."

"Sure. I'm Sonja. The place is a wreck, and from what I've seen, there's not much left here worth taking."

"Thank you, Sonja. My mother asked me to look."

"Go ahead, take your time, I should probably be on my way."

Sonja slips on a black leather jacket, plucks a designer purse off a side table, and hustles over to the front door. She turns around.

"Please lock up, when you leave," she says.

Claire recognizes the young woman comes from wealth.

So, why is Clyde so poor? *Or was.*

"Give your mother my condolences. It's a shame Arthur had to die like he did." And Sonja closes the door behind her.

Alone in the cabin, Claire wonders what she's looking for. She pilfers through an old maple desk. Mostly thumbtacks and dried ink pens. One closet houses Clyde's size twenty clothes. Overalls, flannel shirts, work shoes—one pair with soles covered with red mud.

Claire recalls her mother's poignant confession: *Arthur came home with red mud on his boots and ruined my new rug at the backdoor.*

Somehow, the red mud seems important, like a clue.

Claire continues her search. Someone has cleaned out the fridge and wiped it down so it won't stink. Probably the granddaughter.

Nothing but a shotgun in the second closet.

Dust bunnies crawl under Clyde's queen bed. No sheets on it. The veneer nightstand is empty. There's a landline in the kitchen. But no connection and no phone directory to be seen anywhere.

"Okay," Claire mutters to herself, "I guess this is it."

She locks the cabin door and drives back to the house.

Claire finds her mother on the sofa taking a nap as the washing machine in the laundry room gently swishes the dirty bath towels.

She notices the carpet in the den needs to be vacuumed, but first she'll clean the two bathrooms. Her mama is sleeping soundly.

Just as dusk descends Claire see's Ted's Mercedes out the kitchen window as he parks behind her Buick. Relieved he's here, she opens the backdoor for him. "I'm so glad you're here."

"Hey, honey." He pecks her on the cheek. "How's Mama?"

"She's up now, but took a long nap this afternoon. I think she's putting away the clean towels we washed and dried today."

"I've had a stressful day," Ted complains. "Any alcohol around?" He opens the fridge with the hope of a beer or a bottle of wine. He curses. "I'm sorry, I'm beat with work."

"It's okay, Ted. Stress has been my bedfellow, too."

"So . . ." Ted strips off his suit jacket, "tomorrow we hear what Arthur has left your mother." There are dark circles under his eyes.

"That's the plan," Claire says.

"Is that cherry pie I smell?" He walks over to the counter and removes the foil from the pie pan. "It is. Yum."

"Mama insisted on making it since I ran an errand for her."

Ted shakes the empty coffee pot then looks at his wife.

"What errand is that?"

"She asked me to look around Clyde Willems' cabin and see if one of the keys on Daddy's keyring fit his front door. I still don't know if one does since his granddaughter answered the door."

"Arthur never said anything about Clyde having children."

"I know."

"Ted?"

They both look to the archway separating the den from the kitchen. "How long have you been standing here?" Ted asks.

84

"Not long, I made a cherry pie for you," I tell Ted.

"I found it. Smells delicious, thank you for making it."

I walk over to the coffeemaker. The pot is cold.

"How have you spent the day, Mama?" Ted asks.

"Well . . ." I fill the coffeemaker with water then add ample Columbian to the filter cup, "I pressed the two aprons and eight placemats I made for me and Claire." I look at Ted and note the dark circles under his eyes. He's not getting much sleep.

Is it because I'm monopolizing his wife's time?

"Mama did a beautiful job sewing," Claire complements me. "It seems she's rediscovered an old passion. I suspect Helen and Ben would like to have something homemade from their grandmother."

"Oh, do you think they would?" The idea delights me. "You can ask them what they'd like me to make. I'm good at tablecloths and napkins, not so good at making anything to wear."

Claire smiles and places a hand on my arm.

"Mama, I'm sure whatever you make will be lovely and the children will be grateful. Come Christmas, we'll all get together and celebrate Christ's birthday. You might consider surprising them with your homemade gifts, wrapped in colored tensile and bows."

"Here, at my house," I clarify.

"Or at ours." Claire looks at Ted. "I don't think you need to cook for all of us, it's asking a lot. What do you think, Ted?"

"No, we'll have it here, like we always do," I say.

"Are you sure you're up to a lot of company?" Ted asks.

"You are family, not company. We'll leave a chair vacant at my long dining room table and pretend Arthur is with us. Everyone can bring a dish to go with my turkey and dressing. Of course, I'll make a fresh coconut cake, and I'll have eggnog, sweet tea, coffee."

"Sounds like a plan," Ted says and ventures through the den. As he disappears through the door to the hall, I know he's headed to the guest bedroom to put away his suitcase and work satchel.

I love Ted. I love Claire. I might just love everybody.

But Butch. I don't like him.

A Time to Snoop

16

Friday Night in Nashville

ELLIE SIMPSON IS DRESSED the part of a pimp's eye candy. She finds it exciting to go undercover with the savvy detective that has already won her heart twice over. Wearing a stunning short black dress, silky with a low-cut bodice, a diamond pendant dangles from her slender neck. Due to a tanning salon, she might have stepped off a plane from sunny Florida. "What is it? You're staring at me?"

"What's not to stare at," he teases his secretary.

As Ellie climbs out of the passenger side of Lloyd's Chevy Blazer, she shows plenty of her long legs covered in a net-like black pantyhose. Her blond hair is swept high on her head and held there by a jeweled clasp. He thinks it's a shade lighter than it was this morning, that maybe she went home to dye it again just for tonight.

He kills the motor in the parking lot under a twenty-story high-rise building. The Starlight Lounge is on the top floor.

He gazes at his snazzy date and wonders why he hasn't asked her out on a date before now. He was married twenty years ago and didn't like it. That's why, but today he feels somewhat different.

"Are you ready for this, Ellie? You can back out while you still have time," he says. "But once we go up, there's no turning back."

She nods and winks. "I'm ready."

He leans over and kisses her on the lips. "Thanks, Ellie."

"My pleasure." She feels warm and fuzzy inside all at once.

They go inside the building and ride the express elevator up to the twentieth floor. A guy that looks like a former U.S. Marine stands by the door to the lounge as they exit the elevator.

"Do you have a reservation?" the suit asks.

"No, we just landed in Nashville. Our driver recommended the lounge as a need-to-visit place go get a decent meal," Lloyd replies.

"Go on in," Suit says.

"Thanks." Lloyd mimics a salute.

They pass a male guest, two sheets under the wind, coming out of the Starlight as he wobbles his way to the elevator.

"Well, let's see what this place offers," Lloyd says to Ellie.

The Starlit Lounge is dressed out fancy. Behind a long-curved mahogany bar, four bartenders wearing tuxes take orders, make the specialty drinks, then send pretty women in short black skirts and glittering blouses out to the tables to deliver them to customers.

A few couples prefer to sit at the bar and chat.

"Drinks must be expensive," Ellie comments to Butch.

"We're here to impress, don't worry about it."

A maître d approaches them. "Will you be seated?"

Lloyd answers, "We're new in town, think we'll take a look around if there's no crime in it." He winks at the gay guy.

"No problem, Cutie, take your time." He hands Lloyd a free ticket for two drinks. "Compliments of the management."

Ellie snags the gift cards and stuffs them in her jeweled purse.

"Are we gonna sit and enjoy a drink?" she asks.

Lloyd doesn't answer as he spies a tall, bald black man, possibly Somalian. He is six two, but this giant must be six eight or more. He's muscular built without an ounce of fat on him, probably from regular gym workouts. When he half turns and laughs deeply, Lloyd spies a large diamond stud in one earlobe.

"Who's that guy?" Ellie whispers.

"Slap me," Lloyd tells her.

"What?"

"You heard me. Slap me hard!"

"You're kiddin'." Embarrassment rests in her gaze.

Lloyd turns Ellie around and pinches her butt. Shocked, she spins around and slaps him hard on one cheek.

"Ata, girl!" Lloyd laughs hard.

"Now, go on over there and talk to the big black guy."

"No." Her gaze reflects fear.

"Go on, ask him to buy you a drink. See what he says. Maybe, he tells you something about his life. Go on now, you are undercover, remember?" He points her in the right direction.

Ellie clamps her mouth, and for the road she slaps her boss again. Lloyd frowns and rubs his cheek. She meant to hurt him.

Ellie approaches the giant from the back. "Excuse me?"

He turns around and she looks into the black holes of his sunken eye sockets. He's not young, probably in his fifties.

And scary as hell.

"Hello, pretty lady." He has a European accent.

Ellie gathers courage. "Buy me a drink, I'm in the mood for different company." She frowns at Lloyd.

"Him?" The black giant grins.

Lloyd sees the guy staring a hole through him.

"Didn't you come in with the white skinny guy?"

"Yeah, we need a break from one another." Ellie sighs. "He can be a son-of-a-bitch at times." She's playing her part well.

"Want me to have someone escort him out of here?"

"No, he'll cool down. You have a name?" Ellie looks up and locks her gaze on his face and doesn't let go.

He winks a smile. "I'll tell you mine if you tell me yours first."

"Ellie," she replies. "Ellie Champ." That's her dog's name.

"Well, Ellie, you are certainly a champ all right," he mutters and grabs her by the arm and almost carries her over to the bar.

"John, fix this pretty lady a drink," the giant says. "I need to take this call." He walks away with his cell phone glued to one ear and disappears between the tables as he crosses to the other side.

"And you would be?" John asks, a twinkle in his hazel eyes.

"Ellie Champ." She glanced around to see if Lloyd is anywhere close. He's not and that puts the fear of God and Satan in her.

"Where you from, Ellie?" John tells the bartender to bring two glasses of white wine to the table that a young couple is vacating.

"From all over," Ellie replies. "I'm here with my boyfriend."

"Does he own a name?" John escorts Ellie by the elbow over to the table for two. She sits across from him, far from comfortable.

"He goes by Butch," she replies.

John glances around for an unfamiliar face.

"Well, I don't see Butch anywhere, so I guess it's just us." He winks at Ellie. "Do you live in Nashville?"

"No, Butch and I are just passing through."

"You work?"

"Secretarial, occasionally," she replies.

"How'd you hear about this lounge?"

"Our limousine driver recommended it."

"You know this is a special kind of lounge, right?"

"Special?" Her heart is double-time beating.

"By invitation only. People like to get connected here."

Is he talking about sex? She wonders but doesn't ask.

He laughs hard. "You are an innocent, baby."

"Well, John, why don't you fill me in on the details?"

The glasses of wine arrive at the table.

"I didn't mean to hurt your feelings, Ellie," John says. "To a good time!" He offers a toast. "And possible working relationship."

"Excuse me," Lloyd grabs Ellie by the arm, "she's with me."

"Sure, Ellie was just telling me you were from out of town," John says. "Pull up a chair and let's get to know one another."

"Butch Glover." Lloyd shakes John's hand.

"John Ashbury, co-owner of the Starlight."

"Who's the big black dude?" Lloyd snags a chair from a nearby table and drags it over to John's table where he sits down.

"Here he comes with Sonja, ask him yourself," John says.

Lloyd and Ellie simultaneously turn around and see the black giant with a beautiful white girl heading toward them. She's close to six feet tall, slender and moves lithely like a predator. A few curves in the right places are accentuated by a pair of long lanky legs covered in stretchy leopard fabric. Her loose silky blouse is the exact color of her oversized starlit azure eyes, as pure as shimmering crystals.

The woman is stunningly gorgeous, unforgettable.

"John, who are your new friends?" she asks.

From her accent, Lloyd thinks the beauty is Russian-born.

"Butch Glover." He offers the giant a friendly handshake.

"Dom," the black man replies.

"Good to meet you, Dom. You have an impressive business." The glittering chandelier light reflects off his shiny black skin.

"This is Sonja, my girlfriend," Dom says.

"Nice meeting you, Sonja. This is Ellie, my friend," Lloyd says.

"Where are you from, Butch and Ellie?" Dom inquires.

"I'm a professional gambler," Lloyd answers. "I expect you have additional rooms where guys like me can play cards."

"Not tonight," Sonja says before Dom has a chance to answer. Butch knows she's suspicious of newcomers.

"I understand. You don't know us well enough to trust us. Right, Ellie?" He looks at her. "We'll settle for some good food."

"Excuse me, I need to use the Little Girl's room," Ellie says.

"I'll show you." Sonja leads her across the expansive dining area.

"Where are you staying, Butch?" John asks.

"We just flew in from Miami, no rooms yet."

"I recommend the Marriot," he says. "I'll call a friend who works the front desk and see if I can get you a room for tonight."

"Thanks, John, I appreciate that." Lloyd hopes Ellie is all right.

As Sonja pushes open the swinging door to the restroom, a young girl passes them. She's barely three years past puberty.

"Who's that girl," Ellie inquires.

"Zoey," Sonja replies as she enters a stall and closes the door.

"Does she work here?" Ellie is in the stall next to Sonja.

"No, she's too young to waitress. Zoey answers the phone sometimes, does a little clerical work for me," Sonja replies.

A few minutes, they are standing together at the marble sink vanity looking into a panel of floor-to-ceiling mirrors.

"And Tennessee makes allowances for an underage to work?"

"What Tennessee doesn't know won't hurt them," Sonja says.

Ellie thinks it best to drop the matter.

* * *

Ted is watching a movie on the TV in the den while I sit at the kitchen table with my daughter. Claire has told me about the red muddy clay she found on Clyde's boots earlier today when she searched his cabin. She thinks it has bearing on Arthur's death. I watch as she Googles soil types in Middle Tennessee.

"Have you found anything interesting?" I yawn.

She pauses from her search. "I think that Daddy and Crawford went with Clyde somewhere and got the mud on their boots."

"It makes sense." She turns the computer screen my way.

"There's three types of soil in southern Middle Tennessee." Claire is bent on educating me. "Sand, limestone, and chert."

"What is chert?" I yawn again. It's already ten thirty.

"It's a fine sedimentary rock made of a microcrystalline variety of quartz Si02," Claire recalls from her reading. She's still young and her brain cells function well. "Chert mixed with shale and sand can appear red, brown, green, gray, or black. It's called mud."

"How much of that red stuff is around us?" I ask.

She shows me a map that pinpoints the areas.

"Here, in Murfreesboro going south to the Georgie line. From a little north of Columbia going south through Marshall County," she explains. "Basically, the southern half of Middle Tennessee. The red mud is found on farmland and the muddy banks of creeks and lakes."

"Oh." Our search for where Arthur, Crawford, and Clyde picked up the red stuff on their boots covers too much territory.

"Could they have gone fishing together?" I wonder.

"They were doing something fishy, that's for sure."

I can't help but laugh, though death is far from funny.

"I'm going to give Butch a call on Monday and talk to him about what I found in Clyde's daddy's log cabin and ask about the woman."

"What woman?" This is the first I've heard of a woman.

"Clyde's granddaughter, or so she claimed," Claire replies.

"He never mentioned having children," I recall.

"His granddaughter's name is Sonja and I can describe her in detail to Butch. I want him to find her and see what she knows. With Clyde dead, Butch is surely convinced you are innocent."

"You think he'll take off this blame ankle bracelet?"

"I hope so, Mama. Let's go to bed, I'm tired."

"I'll get the lights." *I surrender to another difficult day.*

A Time for Anger

17

Saturday, November 6th

CLAIRE IS UP SATURDAY morning before I am and is preparing a country-ham breakfast for the three of us. Ted won't be dieting this morning because I'm going to make scratch biscuits.

Don't ask me why they're called that, but I start out with three cups of self-rising white flour, add half a cup of vegetable oil, blend it with my own two hands then add enough buttermilk to mix and pat out on a floured board. I'll cut out the biscuits in rounds, place them on a greased oven pan and bake at 375 degrees for twenty minutes.

I walked past Claire and invade the pantry to collect the flour and vegetable oil. "I'm making homemade biscuits this morning."

"The *scratch* kind?" She flips the salty pork in the skillet.

"Yep, just like your grandmother Lillie used to make for me and my brother." Dennis died three years ago from cancer.

"You realize I bought frozen biscuits the last time I shopped at Kroger," Claire informs me. "They are decent if you don't feel like going to all that much trouble." She swipes her hands on a tea towel.

"Let's pamper Ted this morning," I say. "He thought you were coming home before Mr. Dunwoody set up an appointment today."

Claire smiles. "The meat will be ready shortly, so you better get started." She cracks half a dozen eggs to scramble.

I like my scrambled eggs with cheese and sour cream.

The bread is in the oven baking ten minutes later.

Through the archway between the kitchen and the den, I see Ted watching the morning news. I fix him a cup of coffee and take it to him. He likes it black and strong. "Here, Ted. Enjoy!"

He looks up at me. "Thanks, did you sleep well, Mama."

"Perfect, the sleep med Doc Hammons prescribed is miraculous. I took two, crashed and bingo! It's morning before I knew it."

Ted yawns then sips on the coffee I gave him.

"Maybe Claire and I should get some of those pills. We kicked each other all night and I feel like I'm straight out of a fighting ring."

"Drink your coffee and you'll feel better. Claire almost has breakfast ready. I made scratch biscuits to go with my homemade butter from our lingering cow, and my blackberry jam."

"Well, that sounds like a bang-up country breakfast."

"Biscuits are up!" Claire calls out. "Come and get it!"

We sit at the table. Ted says the blessing over our food. We eat in silence. I have two biscuits and discard any thought of dieting.

As Claire and I clean up the dishes it's almost nine o'clock and Ted goes out to the shed and gathers some of Arthur's tools for his workshop. He likes making furniture and whatnots—most things not good enough quality to use inside his expensive home.

"I'm going to shower and wash my hair," I tell Claire then ask, "Will you run the vacuum over the den rug again?"

"Sure, Mama. You want me to stretch out some of your curls with my hot iron?" She tinkers with my kinky white curls. "One day next week, I'll get permission from Butch to take you over to Gloria's for a haircut." We walk through the den together.

The morning goes quickly and it's eleven a.m. before we know it. I hear a vehicle crunch the gravel outside my house.

"I think Arthur's attorney is here," I inform Claire. I always think of Jacob as Arthur's because up to this point, he had handled all our business dealings. But now, it's *my* time to take charge.

"I need to tell Ted to hurry, he's still in the shower."

"I'll open the door for Jacob and his secretary. You go on and build a fire under Ted. I want to get this will-reading over with."

"Mr. Dunwoody!" I greet him at the front door and invite him and Cynthia into my foyer. "Thank you for coming to the house."

"No, problem, it's a privilege. I haven't been here in a while."

"May I take your jacket?" I query Cynthia.

"No, I'll keep it on for now, Mrs. Powell."

"We'll take care of business at my kitchen table. I don't keep this part of the house warm during winters." I lead the way.

"You have a charming property, Dorothy." Jacob calls me by my first name. He was in kindergarten when I graduated Maury High School. He's no young rooster anymore but he still prances.

"It's been a good place for Arthur and me to live for fifty years. When our grandchildren were younger, they used to love coming out to the farm to ride ATV's over the rugged landscape."

"It's a child's fantasy to be footloose in uncharted territory."

"Can I get you and Cynthia something to drink while we wait for Ted and Claire?" I ask as they take seats at the kitchen table.

"None for me," Jacob answers.

"I'll have a glass of water," Cynthia says.

* * *

Lloyd rolls over in his bed and groans as his head explodes with pain. He feels the mattress shake like someone is lying beside him. He squints his eyes at the sunlight invading his bedroom then reaches for his weapon. "Don't shoot!" he hears Ellie say before he sees her.

He rolls over in the bed to face her.

"You been here all night?"

"Half the morning," she replies.

"Did we——?

"No," she cuts him off. She wishes.

"What time is it?" He shades his squinted eyes from the light.

"One o'clock in the afternoon. Saturday, in case you forgot."

He lets loose a few curse words then apologizes.

"Somebody at the bar must've spiked your drink," Ellie says. "You passed out last night around eleven at the Starlight Lounge. Don't you remember any of this?" She is fully dressed and gets up.

"Some of it, I'm a bit foggy."

"I need a shower."

"Wait, Ellie. What were you doing while I was comatose?"

"Undercovering," she teases. "Sonja pitched a job to me."

Lloyd throws his legs off the bed and forces his body to sit up.

"What kind of job?" He waddles like a duck to the bathroom door then turns around. "Hold that thought."

When the door shuts, Ellie wonders if she should tell all.

* * *

Claire, Ted and I are sitting at my breakfast table that seats eight people—I know, it's bigger than most but I had it custom made decades ago and it's served my family well. I try to focus.

Jacob Dunwoody is reading Arthur's will. I hear his words and watch my daughter's expressions change from joyous to sad as she comprehends her daddy's final thoughts when he leaves this world for another. *Heaven*, I pray. But how can I know for sure?

Am I God? Arthur said he was a Christian. But did he meet all the requirements for followers of Christ? I know he gambled and drank alcohol. *Then who am I to pass judgment?*

Jacob's legal secretary, Cynthia, sits quietly sipping on a glass of water as she listens. He finishes reading and looks up.

"Like you all thought, Dorothy gets the house on two-hundred acres, all the farm implements, the vehicles, and what's currently left in their joint bank account." He looks at Claire and grins.

Is he flirting? I feel my angst rising.

My lovely daughter folds her hands on the table and waits.

"Claire, your daddy left you $100,000 in stocks," he says.

"Wait!" I jump up. "When did Arthur buy stocks?"

Jacob opens his mouth then defers his answer to Claire.

"Daddy told me about the stocks a decade ago, Mama," she explains. "His stock investments have more than tripled during that time." She glances over at Theodore. I'm back to calling him that because I have an idea that he told Claire not to tell me about Arthur's stock purchase. And that makes me hopping mad.

"Mama?"

I look at her, tears in my eyes. "What?"

"You can have the money if you need it."

I get up and walk into the den and try to compose my emotions. *"Double D-D and S-S!"*

I curse aloud and don't care what anybody thinks. It's not about the money. It's about Arthur not trusting me enough to tell me he invested a portion of our savings account in stocks. It takes me two walks around the den to cool down. I'm angry he didn't trust me.

I return to the kitchen. Four faces look at me like I'm from Mars. "I'm not upset that Arthur gave you money, Claire. I'm angry he didn't trust me enough to tell me. I'll never forgive him."

I storm out of the kitchen, practically stumble through the den as I try to run, put one foot before the other as I go down the hall to my bedroom, *not* Arthur's anymore, throw myself across my bed.

"Arthur! You bastard!" I bawl hard.

A Time to Rejoice

18

Sunday, November 7th

YESTERDAY AFTERNOON, TED and Claire left for Nashville soon after Attorney Jacob Dunwoody finished reading Arthur's Will and left for town with his secretary. I recall how upset I was to hear Arthur invested in the stock market and never told me. Claire never said a word, either. But today, I feel some better about it.

Who needs a hundred thousand dollars in stock when I have half a million from Arthur's life insurance policy?

Still, most worrisome, I must figure out what my life will look like going forward. I'm in reasonably good health, sound mind most of the time, so I won't be selling my house anytime soon.

I don't want to move into an apartment complex with a bunch of noisy young people. Or, God forbid, an assisted living facility.

I still know how to write checks to pay my bills. I might even get a credit card. I smile at my bravery. First, I must plan Arthur's memorial service and decide what to do with his cremated ashes.

And I will do it, Arthur. Somehow, with God's help.

I miss Claire and hope she'll forgive me for my childish behavior. Of course, Arthur would want her to have monetary support for her family. She might even share some of the money with Helen and Ben. They can invest it, buy a property, or save it for a rainy day. In this world, there are always rainy days.

I sigh. I'm glad the sun shines brightly today.

After all this thought, I should probably get out of bed.

Sometimes if I think too much, I might not get out of bed at all. I might just lie there and rethink my whole life. My childhood years growing up in a minister's household. God bless my daddy! My career as a biology teacher. The day Arthur came back into my life I fell in love with him all over again. The first time I saw Claire after giving birth. How I felt when Lance died. *Poor Lance.*

I can't think about him now. Time to get moving.

I get up, putter to the hall bath, and turn on the shower. I wait until the pipes shake and the hot water flows before I strip off my pajamas. I step into the stall. There's nothing better than hot water rolling over my achy old body. If I forget to thank God every day for clean, hot water, I am not a good Christian. Which reminds me I should be in church this morning. But I can't. Because of this blame ankle cuff. *Double D-D!* I'm angry at Butch all over again.

* * *

Lloyd never attends church. He's had a beef with God since he was thirteen and his daddy beat him half to death on a Saturday when he stayed out too late Friday night. Lloyd Senior was not a good daddy or a decent human being. He beat his wife until she left him.

Then he started in on his only son, a chip all the old block who turned nasty, too. All of that is old news washed under the bridge.

He's at the station this morning making notes regarding what Ellie told him last night about Sonja Berioski. Apparently, they bonded in some strange way. Ellie is good at undercover work. Lloyd wonders why he hasn't asked her out on a date before Friday night.

Ellie's quite a woman. Her husband left her for a younger woman three years ago. He hadn't known that till last night. He realizes they've somehow bonded. And it feels really good to have a confidante in his life. Someone he trusts to share his thoughts and job difficulties.

Ellie would make a good cop, if she decided to go for it. But at her age, it's doubtful the Police Academy would accept her into their program. He recalls what she told him about Sonja.

"Sonja grew up in Russia. After her mother died from mysterious circumstances, she moved to America with her father. She was ten when they applied for citizenship. Sonja's twenty-nine now and master of her own life."

Ellie looks at Butch.

"Did she say what her father does?"

"No, but I think he's a Russian spy," Ellie reveals.

"Why do you think that?" Lloyd asks.

"Because when I asked her what her father did, she answered, 'If I tell you I'd have to kill you.'" Ellie laughs. *"She stole that expression from an American movie, but it says a whole lot."*

"What kind of job did Sonia offer you?"

"Office work, at the Starlight," she replies.

Lloyd thinks about the idea. *"I might want you to take the job."*

"Who will be your secretary?"

"I can replace a clerical worker, but it isn't easy to find a good spy." He can see Ellie likes the compliment by her smile.

"You want to go to bed?" she asks.

"Are you offering?"

"Yeah, I'm all in for undercover work."

Lloyd feels good inside today. He and Ellie are a couple. If they survive the Mafia, he might ask her to move in with him. Of course, he'll have to fire her and find another secretary. But he doesn't think Ellie will care. *"I love you,"* he recalls her saying.

"I think I love you, too, Ellie." Lloyd is shocked at what he's saying aloud to himself. He should give her a call, invite her to lunch.

* * *

It's middle of the afternoon and I'm bored. I consider going out to the shed to pilfer though Arthur's junk, what's left of it after Ted has removed the tools he needs for his own shop. I put on a jacket because it's cold outdoors. But before I go, the landline rings.

I rush across the kitchen to the other side of the breakfast room and snag the phone on the wall. "Hello!" I'm out of breath.

"Is this Ms. Powell?"

"Yes, Butch, it's me." She recognizes his voice.

"How would you like to shed your ankle cuff?"

"You're going to take it off." *Oh, goody!*

The day has just gotten better.

"When? Tomorrow, at the station?" she hurriedly asks.

"If you're not busy, I can come out to your house now."

"I'm busy waiting for you, so come on."

If I could leap for joy, I would. But arthritis misery has got my knees in knots today so I'm barely creeping around.

"Oh, Arthur!" I hear myself talking to my dead, cremated husband. "If you were only here to share my joy!"

I'm nervous as a cat on a hot-tin roof, I recall the darling actress in an old movie I can't quite pull out of my stunned brain.

I look at the wall clock in the den as I sit in *my* recliner with a Bible in *my* lap and a prayer in *my* thoughts. My, my, I'm being awfully selfish in my thoughts today. Shame on me!

The landline rings again and I wonder if Butch is backing out on his promise. I may not have murdered Arthur but I'm going to kill Butch if he does. I rock forward as I pull the lever to upright the recliner. "I'm coming!" I call out as if the phone can hear me.

Huffing and puffing, I pick up the receiver, "Hello."

"Dorothy, it's Lorene Perkins."

"Lorene!" I say. "Oh, Lorene, I'm so sorry I didn't make it to Crawford's funeral. I feel so bad about it. Was it a nice funeral?"

"Oh, yes. My two boys were there by my side. The Funeral Director played *When I Come to the Garden Alone* while everyone was seated and waiting for the service to begin. Crawford looked better than he has in a long time. The mortician filled out his wrinkled face during the embalming so he would look much younger."

Lorene goes on and on until I finally stop her.

"I don't mean to interrupt, Lorene, but I'm expecting company."

"Oh, who's coming over?"

"Detective Peters. He's going to take off my ankle cuff."

"Oh goody! That's great news. It means you're no longer suspected of murdering Arthur. Oh, I needed to tell you something important." She falls silent. "Give me a second to remember."

"Okay, but hurry," I tell her as the front doorbell buzzes.

"Give me a second while I think what it was."

I look at the time on the wall clock in the den. *2:45 p.m.*

"Lorene, I don't mean to rush you but Butch is here."

"Oh, I know what it was. I found Crawford's iPhone."

"He had one of those new Apple things?"

"I phoned the salesperson that sold it to him last month," she reveals. "I didn't know until this morning that Crawford owned one." She pauses. "Don't you think it's strange he didn't tell me?"

"Everything is strange about this situation, Lorene." The doorbell continues to buzz. "Can you hurry up a little bit and tell me why Crawford's phone is important?" I impatiently ask.

"My daughter helped me open it—you have to have a special code to peek inside one of those techy phones. Heather figured out the code." Lorene is on a roll to give me detailed information.

The doorbell buzzes and I'm afraid Butch will leave.

"Lorene? What has Crawford's phone got to do with me?"

"Well, Heather found an address in his Contact List."

I have no idea what Lorene is talking about.

"It's a Murfreesboro, Tennessee address," she says.

"Okay," I wait to be enlightened.

"Do you think this is where Crawford and Arthur went when they got red mud on their boots?" Lorene finally gets to her point.

"Tell me the address so I can write it down." I lay the receiver on the breakfast table and go over to the kitchen cabinet for a pen.

"Okay, I have a paper and pen, go ahead."

I write down the address as my front doorbell buzzes.

"I have to go, Lorene, Detective Peters is at my front door. Have a nice visit with your daughter and her family. When you get back, we'll go out for a nice lunch in town. My treat."

I hang up before she says goodbye and go to the door.

"Come in, Detective." I won't call him Butch and irritate him.

"Why didn't you answer your door?"

"My friend Lorene was on the phone."

Butch brushes past me like he knows my floorplan well. Then I recall that he does. He searched it sometimes back. A long time ago it seems, but it can't be more than two weeks ago.

"We'll talk in the den," I tell him.

"I'm sorry, Dorothy, about the ankle bracelet."

He sits on the sofa with one leg angled on top of the other.

"It's okay, Lloyd, you've given me a lot to think about."

"I know you didn't kill Arthur. Even if you did, the jury would not convict you due to reasonable doubt. I have evidence now that will prove reasonable doubt, so are you ready to be a free woman?"

"I sure am." I smile at Butch, starting to like him for the first time since Susan passed. I push back in my recliner so he can get to my ankle. *Presto!* He enters a code and the ankle cuff pops open.

"There! You're free to go any place you want now."

"Thank you, Lloyd. I know exactly where I want to go because I have the address written down on a piece of paper in my pocket."

"Well, enjoy your trip, I should go now."

I don't tell him I'm going to see the place where Arthur and Crawford probably picked up red mud on the soles of their boots. The last place they probably went before they were murdered.

The coroner told Lorene her husband died of natural causes, but I think differently now. Crawford was scared to death.

Butch is saying something and I've lost focus.

"What did you say to me, Detective Peters?"

"I said take care, Dorothy."

We're standing at the front door. "You, too!" I smile.

He spins and walks out the door like a peacock with his feathers spread. I suppose it's a milestone to get me out of his hair.

"Have a nice rest of the day, Detective Peters!" I respectively call out to him as he steps off my wrap-around porch into the cold bright November day. And wonder what this afternoon will hold.

After thinking over my plan, I've decided it's not wise for me to drive all the way to Murfreesboro by myself. When Claire returns tomorrow morning, she can drive me. So, I spend the afternoon taking a walk around my property. Just looking at the dying fall foliage and the birds flying overhead going south for warmer weather.

Claire calls me just as it gets dark outdoors.

"How are you making it, Mama?"

"Great! Butch took off my ankle bracelet this afternoon."

"Really? And you didn't call to tell me?"

"No, I didn't want to disturb you and Ted," I say. "I know Helen and Ben probably came over, maybe had lunch with you."

"You're almost correct," she says to me. "Ted and I went to the 10:30 church service at First Baptist this morning and met the kids downtown at Jeff Ruby's Steakhouse for a late lunch."

"Food must've cost a pretty penny," I comment.

"One of Ted's clients gave us a gift card, Mama. Lunch didn't cost us one penny. But you're right, it's a very exclusive restaurant."

I guess she put me in my place.

"Well, I guess you won't be coming here in the morning, since I'm a free woman and can go anywhere I please," I tell Claire.

"I left a few makeup items and some of my clothes in the guest bedroom closet, so I will drive over late morning. If you want, we'll go into town and have a nice lunch at your favorite restaurant."

"Even if it's super expensive?" I tease, knowing Claire is as blessed as I am because Arthur is still taking care of us from the Beyond.

"Sure. My treat," Claire sweetly says. "Oh, and I should check with Mr. Dunwoody to see if he's completed the paperwork required to transfer Daddy's part of the estate to your name alone."

Alone. There goes that dad-blasted word again.

"Okay, Claire, whatever you want," I tell her. "But after lunch I want you to drive me to an address in Murfreesboro."

"Whom do you know in Murfreesboro?"

"It's not *whom* I know, it's *whom* Arthur knew." It tickles me to use perfect English like Claire and Ted. I'm being silly.

"Okay, Mama, sleep well tonight."

"See you tomorrow." I end the call, cut out the breakfast and kitchen lights then go into the den and switch on the television.

I find an old 1960's movie starring Clint Eastwood. It's a shoot 'em up detective flick. The actor was so attractive when he was young. *Weren't we all?* I could float around in his eyes until time ends.

It's a *Dirty Harry* sequel. I sit in my recliner to watch.

A Time to Explore

19

Monday, November 8ᵗʰ

I TOOK A SLEEPING TABLET last night so I'm rested this morning. My ankle is still a little sore but I'm relieved not to be incarcerated in my own house. In fact, I feel like I might run a marathon. Then I rethink that stupid idea. At eighty, I might fall or collapse.

Or worse, die. NO, Arthur still needs my help.

I'm in the mood to clean out closets this morning. I start with the coat closet tucked under the winding staircase to the second floor where I gather all the extra coats Arthur has hoarded for decades.

I check each one for moth holes to see if they are decent enough to donate to the Salvation Army or Goodwill Industries. I remove a long black woolen coat, Size 10, that I'll never wear again.

Which reminds me I am too fat and should diet.

By nine thirty, I've packed four large boxes of Arthur's and my formerly-used clothes—I try not to think old—from the closet under the staircase and the three upstairs bedroom closets. My outfits that are unsuitable for my age and blossoming figure. I'm exhausted.

I'll ask Ted to bring down the boxes when he next visits me.

Worn to a tether, I tramp downstairs and negotiate the hall, trying not to lose my balance. As I open the door to the breakfast room, I bump into Claire. "Where did you come from?"

"I was looking for you, Mama. What are you doing?"

"You startled me." My heart is racing.

"I'm sorry, didn't mean to. What are you up to?"

My daughter is nosy. She likes to keep track of everything I do. She would make a good detective, but I don't think she'd ever arrest me for my disreputable thoughts. I guess I'll answer her question.

"I've been upstairs cleaning out closets and boxing up the stuff Arthur and I will never use again—old coats and clothes that are out of style." I heave a breath. "And now I'm taking a break."

"I put a box of donuts on the kitchen cabinet," she tells me.

"Why? Do I look like I need more fat on this wrinkled body?" I ask a little too harshly and rightly earn her disparaging glare.

"I know . . ." a huge sigh leaks out of me.

"You're too hard on yourself, Mama," Claire says.

I know my intelligent daughter means well, but she is winding up for a speech about how older people have achieved so much in life and how they should be proud of themselves and never disparage the way they look because old age is a consequence of living well.

I sigh at my long, laborious, practically useless thought.

"Are you ready to settle down and rest a bit?" she asks as we walk into the kitchen and she opens the lid on the white box.

"Did you get breakfast this morning?" I query her.

"I had a donut during my drive over," Claire replies.

"What kinds are left for me?" I peek inside the Dunkin box.

"A variety, make us some coffee and we'll pig out together."

I already look like a fat little pig, but I like donuts. And who cares what I look like anyway? I'll never be in a beauty contest again.

While I putter around in the kitchen and make the coffee, Claire checks her email on her fancy iPhone. I can see her clearly through the opening in the wall behind the stove. Arthur cut it out years ago because he couldn't talk to me while I was cooking in the kitchen.

He was always full of questions and wanted to know my opinion on things. Well, he won't be asking me anymore questions now, or telling me what to do for the rest of my days. *Poor Arthur!*

I bet he misses bossing me around. I wonder if God assigns special angels to endure husbands' abuses when they get to Heaven.

Claire put her phone away. "Mama, what's wrong? Are you still mad at me about the stocks Daddy gave me?"

She sees me laughing. "Nothing's wrong, Claire. I feel rested and optimistic this morning." The last of the coffee bubbles out.

"Explain all this optimism, please."

I savor the moment before answering as I fill two mugs with dark Columbian coffee and add ample real cream from my one almost dead cow then say, "I'm a free woman."

She looks down at my ankle.

"You took it off, will you get in trouble?"

"I didn't take it off." I hand Claire her mug. "Detective Butch came out to the house yesterday afternoon and put in the code."

"I hope you were nice to him."

"Butch says even if I killed Arthur no jury will convict me because of reasonable doubt." I thank God for His favor.

"I'm blown away!" Claire exclaims. "That's wonderful news!"

"Not for Arthur. Somebody else murdered your daddy and we need to find out why." I take a sip of my *perfect* coffee and celebrate a *perfect* future where everything turns out for justice when I know who killed my husband. "It's up to us to find his killer."

"Mama, leave it alone. Let the professionals do their job."

Claire plucks a chocolate-glazed donut from the box as I choose two of the blueberry and place on my paper plate. We sit at the table together to pig out and drink our coffees, saying very little.

After cleaning up our mess, Claire offers to help me pack away some of Arthur's summer clothes hanging in the guest bedroom closet. As we work, I feel empowered, like I'm the master of my own destiny—with a little help from God, of course.

We're not hungry at lunchtime but I fix a tuna sandwich anyhow and cut it in half to serve with salty chips.

"Lorene Perkins called me late yesterday." I show Claire the address I wrote down on a piece of paper. "We think this is where Arthur and Crawford picked up the red stuff on their boots."

"Clyde Willems, too." Claire takes the note from me and studies it. "Do you think they saw something that got them in trouble?"

"Maybe something bad enough, it got them killed?"

"Yes," Claire replies.

"Lorene and I agree it's possible."

"I'm going to Google the address and see what comes up."

Claire opens her laptop computer and begins typing. I stand behind her, leaning slightly forward so I can see the screen better.

"It's land that's owned by a corporation," Claire tells me.

"What kind of corporation?" I query.

"An investment firm of some kind, I expect," Claire replies, all the time typing to locate a picture of any structures on the property.

"How much land is there?" I ask.

"Seventy-nine acres south of Interstate 840, somewhere east of Shelbyville but it has a Murfreesboro, Tennessee address."

"Let me see." I lean closer to the screen.

"What are you looking for, Claire?"

"I'm linking the property address to a satellite hookup," she explains. "That way we can zoom in on the property and see if it has structures on it." She types fast as I stand over her and watch.

"You can see something on the ground that a satellite sees while we sit here looking?" I should not be surprised that technology has run so far ahead of me I can't even see its tail. I'm silly as a goose.

"There it is!" Claire turns the screen my way.

"What?" I look hard at the landscape as I sit in a chair.

"There's a building with a creek running beside it." Claire stands behind me. "Well, I do declare—in the famous words of Scarlet O'Hara—I think we're looking at an old gristmill."

She erects her bowed body and stretches.

"There!" I point at the screen, delighted I'm so techy.

"Let's go see for ourselves what's there," Claire mutters.

I stand up, turn around and look at her.

"What? You don't want to see for yourself?"

"And you don't care what Butch thinks?" I counter.

"What he doesn't know won't hurt him," Claire prophesies.

I'm joyful. "When?"

"Now." She shuts down the computer and we put on our coats and sail on out the backdoor with our purses in hand on our way to Wizard Land where goblins are too afraid to go and the Dorothy in the children's story dares not click the heels of her glittering red shoes to take her home. No ma'am, there's too much mystery to explore in the Land of Oz. And we're off to see the Wizard.

A Time for Searching

20

IT'S MID-AFTERNOON, MONDAY, and Detective Lloyd Peters is standing in the lobby of the municipal building where the Captain of Investigation for Maury County has an office. He informs the female manning the front desk that Captain Colbert is expecting him then walks over to the elevator, one of two, and boards it.

It's a quick ride up, a show of progress gifted by federal taxpayer funds. But he's not complaining. He gets off on the third floor.

"Detective." Marilyn greets Lloyd with a fist bump. Influenza has broken out in Middle Tennessee so folks are careful not to spread germs. "I presume you have information for me." She's all business.

"I wanted to personally give you a report concerning what I've learned regarding Arthur Powell's murder and other related cases."

Lloyd takes a seat as Marilyn motions to him.

"So, you see a connection between the recent murders, two in Maury County and one in Dickson. You were in Nashville Saturday evening with your secretary—Eleanor, isn't it? And snooped a bit?"

"She snooped a lot, not so much me, since I was drugged."

Lloyd notes Marilyn's lips rise in one corner, a half smile.

"Did you find Mark Hagen?" Clyde Willems' younger half-sister told Lloyd that his contact with the Mafia was Hagen.

"No, we didn't see him there," Lloyd reports. "But we met John Ashbury, and the owner, Dom—he didn't give a last name. Dom's a huge Somalian with black holes for eyes. A pretty imposing figure."

The Captain mulls over Lloyd's comment.

"Captain," Lloyd continues, "I believe that Dom's legitimate bar-and-restaurant business is a coverup for a more lucrative prostitution empire he operates with the help of his girlfriend."

"Who is?" Marilyn alerts to new information.

"Sonja Berioski is the name she gives, but it may be bogus."

"All their names may be bogus, Detective." Marilyn think about how to proceed going forward. "I think we need FBI involvement."

"Wait, there's another angle to this equation."

A question mark rests on the dark face of the Captain.

"Sonja offered Ellie a job in the office at the Starlight Lounge. She thinks we're new in town and looking to earn some cash."

"Eleanor is a secretary and not trained for undercover work."

"She's a natural. I don't think it would hurt for her to call Sonja and accept the job, work a week, and see what turns up."

"I'll need to deputize her for undercover work."

Lloyd grins. "Ellie would love that, trust me."

* * *

It's almost three p.m. on Monday as Claire drives me in her Buick toward the clandestine destination, acreage that supports an old gristmill located south of the 840-E interstate exchange between Shelbyville and Murfreesboro. It's begun to mist a fine sleet.

"Weather's going to turn nasty later tonight," Claire says.

I'm more interested in how we will fare, not the weather.

"What if we run into trouble?" I ask. "You think we should call Butch and tell him what we're doing?" I'm in no mood to die today.

"We won't get close enough to the gristmill for anyone to see us, Mama." My Claire is in a detective mode to thrash out the red mud clouding our understanding of what really happened to her daddy.

"I have a pepper spray gun," I confess.

"Spray won't do us much good against a spray of bullets."

Now I am convinced Butch ought to know what we're doing.

"No," Claire reads my mind, "we aren't calling Butch until we know we have something concrete to tell him."

She already sounds like a detective or one of those crime-scene specialists that analyzes data at a murder scene. I sigh. We've both watched far too many C.S.I. type shows on television.

Claire glances at the visual map on the dashboard.

"Looks like we're getting off on the exit to Shelbyville. We'll pass through town and I hear a new coffee shop has opened with divine specialty drinks. What about it, Mama?"

"Sure, a hot latte sounds good." I shiver more from the unknown than from the drafty cold wind skirting around the windowsills.

We drive another thirty minutes until we're circling town square.

"Is that it?" I point to Sally's Coffee Lounge.

"Yes," Claire replies. "It appears Sally encourages people to hang out there with their laptops. I suspect students like to fraternize with friends during after-school hours and on weekends while enjoying a specialty coffee with desserts. I always did as a teen."

"You do now." I laugh.

"I know some rural areas of Tennessee still don't have good wi-fi connections. I hope we can find a vacant table where we can sit."

"It would be nice to enjoy a snack in a peaceful atmosphere."

"Did you forget young folks don't do peace?" I chuckle.

Claire finds a parking space on the opposite side of the square from Sally's. We get out of the car and she locks up. It's sleeting harder now and I'm not wearing a heavy coat for our excursion.

The shop is not as full of patrons as we anticipated. We find a vacant table near the back of the old brick building with high ceilings, and I'm reminded of a Starbuck's in downtown Jackson, Tennessee.

A tall, lean senior woman with stark-white hair approaches us.

"Good afternoon, ladies, I'm Sally." She flashes a winsome smile. "I own this wreck, so what can I get'cha?"

"Where are all the lounging students?" I inquire.

"There's some kind of fair going on at the high school this afternoon to raise funds for new uniforms for the basketball teams."

I listen to the quiet and it's nice. Only delicious odors.

"What's your best specialty coffee?" Claire asks Sally.

"A salted caramel with a twist of cocoa and a tinge of almond. I guarantee you will love it, or it's on the house." Sally chuckles.

"Sounds good to me," Claire says, "and bring two scones."

"What kind?" Sally inquires.

"Almond," Claire replies.

"And for you, young lady?" Sally looks at me.

She's already my best friend. "I want the salted caramel."

When Sally hustles off to fill our orders, I tell Claire, "Maybe I should open up a coffee lounge in Columbia that caters to both adults and students." I'm really liking the idea.

"At eighty years old? Why would you, Mama?"

"Because I can, and because I'm rich."

"*Almost rich*," Claire reminds me. "Attorney Dunwoody hasn't finalized the paperwork and electronically transferred the funds to our bank accounts." She places a warm hand over mine.

"Then we should call and inquire," I suggest. "Will we need to sign some official documents?" The wind whistles outdoors.

"Possibly." Claire gazes out the front window. "We'll talk to Jacob tomorrow and see if he needs anything else from us."

In our hometown, most folks have known one another since childhood. Some have grown up and left the area while a few more have drifted in to put down roots. So, longtime residents find it difficult to call someone by their professional title when they've known them all their lives by their first names. I sigh.

Why am I thinking about this now?

"The weather's getting worse, we should go home," I tell Claire. I know when we're beat and should retreat to safety.

"Not until I've had my coffee and seen the old gristmill."

"We can come back another time," I suggest.

Imagine, I'm the reasonable one.

"No, first we will complete our search."

"Claire! Be reasonable. It's starting to snow hard."

"We'll take a quick look and go home. I'll spend the night with you," Claire says. "I don't want to drive home in the snow and in the dark." It is an ominous statement and scares the willies out of me.

* * *

Lloyd is back at his office by four fifteen. The thick cloud coverage has turned the day even darker. Ellie's seated at her desk, looking beautiful and sexy now that he considers her his girlfriend.

She glances up and holds his stare. "What's up, Boss?"

"You're fired!" He walks past her desk and goes into his office and slams the door. Then waits for his comment to register.

She'll resist. A nanosecond later, the door opens and Ellie stands there. "You are incorrigible, Detective! You can't fire me! I know far too much about you and if I talk to the media you won't like it."

111

Lloyd leans back in his swivel chair and rocks a bit, his hands behind his head, amused at her spunk. He waits for her fury.

"Dammit, Butch! I refuse to be fired!"

His boots plop as they hit the floor.

"Better hear my reason first."

She's blinks those amazing green eyes.

"You're fired since Captain Colbert is about to deputize you for an undercover assignment," Lloyd informs Ellie.

"I don't understand." Her lips are weirdly crunched.

"You're going to accept that sleezy job Sonja Berioski offered you at the club." Lloyd's lips quiver as he denies the urge to laugh.

"What?" His statement registers.

Ellie walks up to Butch and slaps him hard.

"I hate you, Lloyd Peters!"

He grabs her, backs her against the door, and passionately kisses her. "Go ahead and hate me, I think I love you," he confesses.

The next few minutes are for only behind closed doors.

When Ellie is seated at her desk again, her face glowing pink, she tells Butch, "I forgot to tell you I recognized someone at the Starlight Lounge." She resumes typing and he knows she's teasing him.

"Who, Ellie?" He grabs her hand so she can't type.

"The girl that passed me and Sonja when we went into the restroom," she replies. When he starts to close the computer, she slaps his hand. "Stop it, Butch! I have to earn my paycheck."

"Do you know the girl's name?"

"I'll tell you when I finish this report."

Lloyd lowers the lid to the laptop. "Now, Ellie."

"Stop it, Boss, I'm working." She opens her laptop.

"Woman! Am I gonna have to shake the info out of you?"

"Done!" Ellie shuts down her computer. "Go ahead, shake some info out of me, Boss. The fight might turn out to be fun."

A Time for Helping

21

IT'S AFTER HOURS AT the high school, too late to ask the principal permission to see the yearly annuals going back five years. Ellie recalls the public library also has copies, so that's their destination.

"It's amazing what you can learn about a person from their yearbook," Ellie tells Lloyd. "I might look you up, what year?"

Not answering her, he's pulling into the library parking lot.

"Stay focused, Ellie, this quest is not about me."

"I am focused. On you," she teases.

There's a glow on Ellie's face and a light in her eyes that tells Lloyd he won't be spending the night alone. He parks as close to the front door as he can and they exit his Chevy. It's snowing hard and the amber pole lights have popped on to dispel the darkness.

"Looks like the library is still open," Lloyd tells Ellie as they approach the front door. He politely opens it for her.

Mrs. Lucy Pennetta, a transfer from New Orleans following Hurricane Katrina, sits at the main desk typing on her computer.

"Excuse me." Lloyd grabs her attention.

Lucy looks up, surprised to have guests on such an awful night.

"The library's closing at five today, just so you know," she says.

"No problem, we won't be here long."

Lloyd knows Lucy has never forgiven him for arresting her son for drug possession three years ago. When you are an officer of the law, even good people try to protect their territories.

"We need to see some high-school annuals," Ellie announces.

"Oh. Sure." Lucy stands up and glances around. "I don't see Donna anywhere, but I can show you where we keep the yearbooks."

"Thank you, Lucy." Lloyd calls her by her first name. He can see her feathers ruffle like a mad hen and feels somehow rewarded.

They follow the pencil-thin librarian through a maze of tall bookcases that contain written information about almost everything in the world from the history of humanity to the present.

Ellie notes the numerous romance and science-fiction novels lining the shelves. It's reported crime novels sell best on Amazon. Go figure. They reach their destination when Lucy stops.

"Here they are," she tells Ellie, not acknowledging Lloyd.

"Thanks, Lucy," Lloyd cannot resist saying.

Meanwhile, Ellie grabs a stepstool and climbs up to the top to view the dates printed on the front of the annuals.

"I'll pass them down to you," she tells Butch.

"Do you need me for anything else, Ellie?" Lucy inquires.

"No thank you, we won't be long."

"Remember five o'clock, the library closes."

"Yes, ma'am," Ellie replies respectfully.

As soon as Lucy disappears around the corner of a bookcase, Ellies fusses at Butch. "You need to be nice to Mrs. Pennetta."

"When hell freezes over, we might make amends."

Ellie is not surprised, so she offers no response.

Butch carries a stack of yearbooks to a rectangular table and spreads them out, then sits down. This is Ellie's project.

She starts flipping through the pages of the oldest annual, looking hard at pictures and names, occasionally reading some of the comments. "Politicians sometimes get in trouble for what friends in high school write about them," she says. "Did you know that?"

"Stay focused, Ellie, we don't have long till five o'clock."

She moves on to the next annual and the next. They have been looking at pictures for twenty minutes when Ellie points to one.

"*Her!* I'm sure of it." She stands up and stretches. "I need a glass of wine. My shoulders are so tight they might snap."

Lloyd massages her shoulders. "Drinks and supper are on me." He studies the pretty student from last year's annual. A junior then. She has pretty brown eyes and hair as shiny as a black filly.

Ellie stacks the books so Lloyd can carry them back to the shelf.

"Zoey Jackson," he reads her name aloud then recalls the high school janitor has the same last name. "Ellie?" He glares at her. "Do you think she's Donald Jackson's granddaughter?"

"I don't know, Butch, let's put these annuals back."

They walk around the corner of the bookcase and Ellie climbs upon the stool to shove the annuals back in their proper space.

Down on the floor again and safe, Ellie looks at Butch.

"All done, now what? Drinks, I hope."

"Let's get an address for Donald and go there," Lloyd decides.

"In all this bad weather?" Ellie is hungry and weary.

"Come on, sport, you're my sidekick solving a crime."

Ellie twists her lips with indecision.

"Okay, let's get out of here." She thanks Lucy Pennetta for her help as they pass by the front desk and head out into the miserably cold snowy weather. The temperature has dropped fifteen degrees.

As they get into the Chevy, Ellie comments, "You can forget about global warming, November will break all cold records."

Lloyd knows Ellie's sweater won't keep her warm so he turns up the heat while she Googles Donald Jackson's home address.

"Here it is, drive and I'll direct you," Ellie says.

Lloyd thinks she's probably going to direct him the rest of his life if it turns out their feelings for one another persist.

Donald's clapboard house is located in a section of town where old homes have undergone renovations. Built back in the 1960s, most are three-bedrooms, two baths, with eight-foot ceilings.

The school janitor's house looks like a paintbrush hasn't touched the siding in twenty years or more. Lloyd parks the truck on the street out front and kills the motor. "Let's see what's inside?"

"Oh joy, I can't wait," Ellie replies as her stomach grumbles.

She hops out of the car and runs up to the front door to knock.

"Wait, Ellie!" Lloyd calls out too late, afraid of what she'll encounter behind the closed door. Before he reaches the stoop, the door opens and the same lovely young girl pictured in last year's annual stands there. One cheek is bruised and her eyes are red.

"Are you Zoey Jackson?" Ellie asks.

"Who wants to know?"

She's an angry teen and obviously abused.

"Detective Lloyd Peters." He shows Zoey his badge. "This is my secretary, Ellie. We're not here to cause trouble, can we talk?"

"About what?" She guards the door.

"Look, I can get a search warrant and come back," he says. "Or we can do this the easy civil way. What about it?" Lloyd waits.

"No, it's fine. Come on in out of the cold." Zoey leans out the door and looks both ways down the street then locks the door.

Lloyd and Ellie enter the house.

"Sorry about all the clutter." Zoey's toasty-brown eyes skitter to Ellie. "Have a seat if you can find one. My grandfather isn't here."

"No problem, we came to talk to you," Lloyd says.

Ellie recognizes a hoarder lives here. Newspapers and unlabeled boxes are stacked around the perimeter of the compact living room, far too hot since the heat is coming from a burning fire inside the old iron stove installed where a fireplace was meant to be.

"Who hurt you, Zoey?" Lloyd asks.

"Why are you here, Detective?"

"To talk, just like I said. Is Donald your grandfather?"

Ellie notes the living room furniture is worn out and filthy with layers of grime. The foul odors crawl all over her skin. She imagines cooties invading her long blond hair and shivers.

"Zoey, if you tell me the truth, and I'll know if you're not, we'll get our answers and leave, I promise." He waits for her to decide.

The teen doesn't care about the dirt as she sits down on the dusty sofa. "Yes, Donald is my daddy's daddy. Hank is serving time in prison." Zoey calls her daddy and grandfather by their first names, which tells Lloyd that she has little respect for them.

Ellie is hopeful Zoey will cooperate.

"My secretary here tells me she saw you at the Starlight Lounge this past Saturday evening. Do you work for Dom?" he asks.

"I do work for Sonja," Zoey admits.

"What kind of work?" Ellie asks.

"I give Sonja the names of the girls I know who need work," the teen replies. "And I keep some books for her on weekends."

"Books with records of girls they hire out as prostitutes?"

Zoey looks a Lloyd, conflicted. "If I tell you the truth, are you going to arrest me and send me to that awful prison like Hank?"

"That's not going to happen, Zoey," Lloyd guarantees.

"My grandfather doesn't know about my job."

Ellie relaxes. "That's good to know since he's employed by the Board of Education to oversee the cleaning of the high school."

"Who slapped you, Zoey?" Lloyd asks again.

"Mr. Hagen," she replies.

"Mark Hagen?" Lloyd wants clarification.

"I don't know his first name. He's a friend of Mr. Clyde—the one that got murdered," Zoey says. "I'm scared they'll kill me, too."

For the first time, Lloyd touches Zoey lightly on her shoulder.

"Whoever *they* are, Zoey, they won't have the chance to kill you because you're coming with us when we leave here."

Zoey visibly wilts and rolls into a knot as she cries hard.

"Now," Lloyd says when her tears have stopped flowing, "start from the beginning and tell us everything you know about Mark Hagen and his associates at the Starlight Lounge."

As he turns on his iPhone recorder, Ellie gives up standing and sits in a wooden rocker, the lesser of evils. Outdoors, it's snowing harder and the night is very dark and very cold.

Zoey's testimony takes another thirty minutes.

Lloyd cuts off the phone recorder and looks at Zoey. "Do you need to pack some things to take with you?"

"Should I?" Her eyelids are limp from fatigue.

"Yes, you won't be back here anytime soon," Lloyd tells her.

"Yes, sir," she respectfully replies, stands up, and stares. As if she's disoriented and doesn't know where to begin the process.

"Get everything that's important to you, Zoey. We'll go shopping later if you need anything else," he says.

"You promise I'll be okay?" Zoey needed reassurance.

"I promise," Ellie chimes in. "We'll keep you safe."

"Go on, Zoey. Hurry up and pack a bag," Lloyd urges.

"Should I leave Donald a note?" she asks. "He might worry."

"Up to you, but don't say anything about coming with us."

Ellie feels sorry for Zoey. Based on the date of the yearbook featuring her picture, she should be a senior graduating next May.

"I wonder if Zoey dropped out of school," Ellie says to Lloyd while Zoey is in her bedroom packing. "This would be her senior year. If so, maybe she can take the G.E.D and graduate."

"It depends on her grades," Lloyd says. "We'll ask."

The room grows silent and cooler as the fire dies down and they wait for Zoey to return. "Ellie?" Lloyd looks at his secretary.

"What, Butch?"

"Be careful not to criticize Zoey, we don't want to make an enemy out of our best witness to a crime syndicate that preys on young girls." He pops his knuckles, anxious to get going.

* * *

Though it's after dark, Claire is determined to make one pass by the old gristmill where it's believed her daddy and Mr. Perkins picked up red mud on their boots. Darkness feels almost deadly as they drive through the wooded countryside between Shelbyville and Murfreesboro. Even the sideroads have become hazardous.

"Mama," Claire speaks, "I think you were right. We should abandon our quest to find the old gristmill in the dark."

"You don't have to convince me it's time to go home."

"The interstate will be coated with a thin layer of ice holding the piling snow in place. Pretty soon the roads will not be drivable."

Nothing new under the sun, we should have started home and hour ago. It's cold in the car with the heat running full blast.

"Not yet," Claire changes her mind. "We're real close. My GPS says it's only three more miles before we turn off."

"Okay then, let's drive by the mill once then go home," I tell Claire. "But if we get stuck in red mud and freeze to death, it's your fault, not mine." I squint to see through the windshield wipers.

"Okay, it's all on me, ye of little faith."

We end up on a gravel road that's half muddy. *Red* muddy.

Oh, goody! I already feel closer to the truth.

A truck rumbles toward us down the half-snowy, half muddy gravel road. When it passes, Claire takes her foot off the gas pedal.

She brakes and turns around for a second look. "Damn!"
"What?" My daughter never curses. She considers it a bad sin.
"That was Sonja, Clyde's granddaughter."
This is stunning news. The plot thickens.

A Time for Independence

22

Tuesday, November 9th

I TURN OVER IN THE BED and look out my bedroom window at the snowy white landscape. As sunlight kisses the naked limps of trees, it turns them into sparkling jewels. I think I'm standing at the doorway to Heaven and Arthur is beckoning me to come inside.

I kick off the covers. "I can't come right now, Arthur."

I willfully force my long legs over the edge of the bed, stand up, then bend over to look for my house slippers under the bed.

"Good morning, Mama."

"Oh." I erect my wobbly body and face the doorway. "Claire! You scared me for a moment. I forgot you spent last night."

I'm reminded it is Tuesday all day long.

"If the snow melts later today I need to go home." She stares at me. "Now that you're free to wander, do you still need me here?"

"No, I can take care of myself, Claire." I tug on a housecoat that's too tight and promise myself I'll diet after Thanksgiving.

No, make that Christmas. *No*, the first of the year is better, I don't want to miss all the great holiday recipes friends prepare.

"Are you sure, because I can stay another night?"

"I'm sure, and I know Ted misses you."

Claire chuckles. "He wouldn't survive in this maddening world without a wife, or a maid, to serve him. In some ways I am both, but I don't mind, he brings home the bacon every month."

I know she's talking about the big check Ted earns from the wealthy country-music stars he legally represents.

"Did you get breakfast already?" I shuffle toward the door.

"No, I was waiting for you, but the coffee's ready by now."

"Then let's go get some."

We walk through the den together. This morning feels like every other day for the last fifty years in this house, but it's definitely not. Arthur isn't here and he never will be. I try to focus as Claire speaks.

"Have you looked outside at the beautiful snow, Mama?"

"I saw it yesterday." We arrive in the kitchen.

"I remember how I used to play in the snow," Claire says.

"Then why don't we do it again?"

"Tromp around in the snow?" Claire looks surprised.

"Sure. After breakfast, we'll put on rubber boots and tromp around in the fluffy white stuff. I did it all the time when I was young. Sledded down hills too. That time in my life was good."

The coffeemaker finishes its job.

We fix our coffee in mugs just like we like it with ample cream and go sit at the breakfast table. Claire fondly pats my hand.

"I'm sure life will be good again, Mama."

I shake my head. "Not the same way it was."

"No, Mama, not in the same way," she agrees.

"What if I don't like the new way?"

"Daddy never took trips overseas, Mama." She clasps my hand. "Maybe Ted and I will plan a trip to Italy and you can go with us."

"Will he mind if I tag along? I walk slower and will cramp your style." I think of all the beautiful scenery I've seen in magazines.

"If Ted doesn't want to go, we can still go."

I open my mouth and close it. Then say, "Really?"

"I'll make Ted not mind or I'll refuse to cook for him."

I laugh at Claire then she laughs, too. We are silly gooses this morning with farfetched ideas that probably never will pan out.

After a light breakfast of toast and fruit—I'm on a diet for at least one day with Claire—we put in a load of dirty clothes to wash.

We are dressed for the cold weather and go outside to wade around in the deep snow covering my backyard. I'm the first to throw a snowball, but Claire is quicker than me and covers me with icy balls that hit my heavy parka and melt down my warmer body.

"Enough!" I cry out in defeat, glad that the sun is bright and melting the snow fast. "Have you checked the weather report?"

We stand on the porch stamping snow from our rubber boots and shaking off what's left of the white covering our warm parkas.

"Fifty-four degrees by two o'clock," Claire informs me.

"Good." I smile as we go inside the house. "I'm going to town this afternoon and talk to Butch in person. Tell him what we know."

"I agree," Claire says.

The morning passes quickly as we take care of some house chores. After eating a sandwich with chips for lunch, we drive to Columbia in Claire's Buick and she parks in the handicapped space in front of the station. From her expression, I prepare for a lecture.

"Now, Mama, be careful not to say anything that will incriminate you," she warns. "You're a free woman and let's keep it that way."

"You don't think I should tell Butch what Lorene and I said to our card friends when Crawford and Arthur brought red mud on their boots into our clean houses and messed up our rugs?"

Two dead on Crystal Creek, I recall.

"If you say that, Mama, I'll arrest you myself."

"I'm not stupid, Claire." I give her my sternest look.

We enter the station and sign the guest register. "We're here to see Detective Peters," Claire tells the rooky female officer.

She checks with his secretary first.

"Ellie says to come on up," the cop reports.

We step on an elevator that takes us up to the second floor. There are three floors in this concrete building, the only attractive feature about the exterior is the American flag out front.

Why am I studying on this and wasting my thoughts?

"Good afternoon, ladies," Ellie politely greets us.

"We're here to see Detective Peters," I tell her.

"He's not here." I get Ellie's sternest look.

My bad, I think of a show I once saw on TV.

"When do you expect Lloyd back?" Claire inquires.

"Fifteen minutes tops, can I get you something to drink?"

"No thanks," Claire answers for both of us.

I read the newspaper while Claire thumbs through a magazine that features overseas trips, and I think she's serious about a vacation.

Butch comes through the door caring a paper carton with two lattes from Dunkin Donuts. "Hello, Claire. Mrs. Powell."

He hands Ellie a Styrofoam cup and smiles at her. He's sweet on Ellie, I can tell, and almost hear wedding bells sounding.

"We need to tell you some things we found out that might help you find Daddy's killers," Claire says right off.

Butch looks at me like I'm causing trouble.

"Can we talk privately in your office?" Claire asks him.

"Sure." He looks at Ellie and winks. "Hold my calls."

"Yes, Boss." She winks back.

I see there's more to their relationship than professional, but I'm glad somebody has the gumption to put up with his arrogant pride.

"Have a seat, ladies." Lloyd closes his office door.

Claire sits down and looks at me. "You go first, Mama."

"What have you done *now*, Mrs. Powell?"

"Did you really think I trust you enough to solve Arthur and Crawford's murders without my help? Poor Clyde Willems, too."

Not a happy camper, he sits up straight and glares at me.

"Okay then, Dorothy, what do you know?"

He drags out my name and I want to spit in his face. Nevertheless, this is business so I start my story a couple weeks back—which seems more like months—and tell him about the red mud Arthur and Crawford picked up on the soles of their boots.

"Arthur ruined the rug at my backdoor and Crawford stained Lorene's den carpet. We were both hopping mad." I look at Claire and she's shaking her head, so I stop there. *Just the facts, ma'am.*

Butch cracks his knuckles. "I see no relevance to a crime."

"Well, you will soon," I'm on a roll. "Lorene Perkins found an address in Crawford's iPhone contact list she didn't recognize. She's in Kentucky visiting her daughter, in case you don't know. She called and gave me the address of the property in the contact list."

Wickedly staring me down, he waits for revelation.

"I wrote it down." I hand Butch the sacred piece of paper.

"Yesterday, Claire and I drove out to an old gristmill in a snowstorm to see for ourselves what was there that interested

Crawford. Of course, we assume Arthur went with him since they both came home the same day with red mud on their feet."

"Is there a point to your story, Dorothy?"

He is trying to irritate me and succeeding.

Claire takes over from there. "Last week I went over to Clyde Willems' daddy's old cabin to see if one of Daddy's keys on his big keyring fit Clyde's front door. But I didn't get a chance to open it."

Butch has his butt in a twist but at least he's listening.

"Clyde's granddaughter opened the door for me," Claire says.

The door opens and Ellie looks in. "He has a granddaughter?"

I stand up and point my finger at Butch. "Isn't it illegal for your secretary to listen to our conversation when we specifically told you it was a private conversation for your ears only?" I gasp at my boldness in a police station and notice the horror on Claire's face.

"Ellie." Lloyd shakes his head. "I got this."

"Yes, sir." She backs out of the office and closes the door.

"She says her name is Sonja," Claire tells all of it.

Butch looks like he's seen a ghost. "Sonja Berioski?"

"She never told me her last name," Claire replies. "But we passed her on our way to view the old gristmill property."

"So, Sonja has been at Clyde's cabin, and to the property where you believe Arthur and Crawford got red mud on their boots."

"Focus, Detective," I say. "You might learn something."

Butch is not talking to me. He's processing our information.

"Don't you think that's suspicious, Detective Peters?" I call him by his official title because we need something from him.

"Mama and I want you to get a search warrant for the old gristmill and the vacant house not far from it," Claire says. "There's plenty of red mud to go around at the address. Maybe Daddy and Mr. Perkins saw something there they should not have seen."

"Maybe Clyde took them there," I add to Claire's statement.

Butch picks up the phone. "Ellie, come in here."

"Look, ladies, there's a lot more to this story than you might imagine. If you are right, I will not only find out who killed Arthur, I will bring down a crime syndicate operating out of Nashville."

"What kind of crime syndicate?" Claire jerks as she asks.

124

"Rather not comment further," Butch says. "Ellie is helping me find out more. She's been deputized by Captain Marilyn Colbert who heads up investigations in the Maury County Police Department."

I look at Butch and wonder why I haven't been deputized. Claire and I have done half the work to solve the crime.

"Okay then," I say.

"You should go home ladies and keep quiet about this conversation. Let us professionals do our jobs. If we learn anything new about Arthur's death, I'll phone you with an update."

"Can I go home with my daughter to Nashville?" I ask.

"Sure. Ellie writes down Claire's iPhone number.

Then Butch addresses Claire. "I may need to interview Theodore," he says. "I know he represents some powerfully wealthy people in Nashville who may have heard something."

"Something?" Claire flashes her blue eyes at him. "What?"

"Claaaire." He drags out her name in an infuriating fashion.

Uh oh, I think he's about to get a dose of my daughter's temper.

"You know, Butch," Claire is speaking at a whisper. "I never said a word about the time you tried to rape me."

Swallowing a curse word, I stand up. "When was that, Claire?"

Butch's face is red as a strawberry's and I can tell Ellie wants to punch him in the gut. I want to do more than that, but murder is against the law. I have to admit, this is the most fun I've had all day.

"Oh, is that so?" Claire isn't finished. "You've forgotten the time I missed the school bus my freshman year and you were nice enough to pick me up before I froze my butt off? Instead you parked on the side of the road and felt me up and down."

Boy, I never knew Claire had so much boldness in her.

"Claaaire . . ." Butch is saying, "I was just checking to see how much woman you were." At his comment, Ellie promptly slaps him.

"You bastard!" She walks out of the office, gathers her coat and purse and leaves through the front door.

Uh oh, Butch is in love trouble.

"Well," I actually smile, "that was interesting, something new under the sun I didn't know." Life going forward will not be boring.

A Time to Reflect

23

I ASK AS WE GET IN CLAIRE'S BUICK, "Are we going home now?"

Not answering, obviously mad, she pulls the car into the flow of traffic on Third Street. As we drive, I notice remnants of yesterday's snow crouching in the deep pockets of the city's buildings where sun light cannot touch. I wonder what Claire's hashing out in her mind.

"First, I want to swing by Jacob Dunwoody's office and find out when he'll be finished with probating Daddy's will," she speaks.

"It's after five, do you think he's still there?"

"We'll find out. His line was busy earlier this afternoon. I've left him two messages to call me. Perhaps we're a nuisance and he's tending to other business he deems more important." Claire sighs.

I can see she's still irritated at Butch, and is taking it out on Jacob. I can't believe that pipsqueak attacked my daughter when she was fifteen and I never knew about it. And now he's a law officer?

His mother Susan would roll over in her grave if she knew.

"Mama, when you get this quiet, I worry." Claire turns down another street. Jacob's office is located in a building on Fourth.

"I was thinking of Butch, when he was in high school, what a young rebellious teen he was, and how Susan put up with it."

"Well, perhaps Butch learned his lesson young and has changed his ways," Claire says and I know she feels bad for stripping down his pride in front of Ellie. Whatever he has going with his secretary might be coming to an end. "There's Jacob's new Rolls Royce."

"Where?" I squint my eyes and realize I may need glasses.

"Look, he's backing out into the street!" Claire exclaims.

She breaks in front of the driveway and startles Jacob.

Recognizing it's Claire honking at him, he turns off the engine, gets out of the car, and walks over to my side of the Buick.

I lower the electronic window. "Hi, Jacob."

"Dorothy." He tips his head slightly in a show of respect. "Can I help you and Claire with something today?"

Claire leans my way. "Mr. Dunwoody, we wanted to ask you if Mama and I need to sign anymore paperwork before you transfer Daddy's funds to our bank accounts?" She waits for his answer.

Nearly in my face, I can smell his cigar breath and know he's recently smoked in a no-smoking building. Probably the cigar is the expensive kind since he drives an expensive vehicle.

"Have you talked to the funeral director about setting a time for Arthur's memorial service?" Jacob asks Claire, not me. "As the executor, I need copies of the paid bills before I can't finalize his will." He pats the rib of the window. "Let me know."

"Thanks, Jacob," I say. "We will get back to you."

Claire pulls away from the curb too fast, an indication she's still irritated. She maneuvers through town until we're on the main highway heading to my house. I don't know how to comfort her.

"Are you ready to memorialize Daddy?"

"I guess, not really." I sigh. "I'd like to tell Arthur we found his killer before I say goodbye and put him in the ground. Or, since he's packed away in a fancy urn, I might scatter his ashes somewhere."

"Mama, I know this is difficult, and you've been a trooper, but we need to take care of this and move on with our lives," she says with a hitch in her voice, and I know she's grieving, too.

"Okay, I'll call Blake Johnson tomorrow and schedule a time for the service next week. I want to put an announcement in the newspaper so friends who want to honor Arthur can attend."

I realize I need to locate several photographs of him so a video can be made of his life through the years and played at the service.

"We'll have a reception following the memorial service in the funeral homes' recreation room," Claire says. "I'll order iced cupcakes from the bakery and we'll serve punch and coffee. We don't have to be sad now that Daddy is in Heaven with Jesus." She peers at me. "I don't want to feel sad anymore. I refuse to be sad."

All the words in the world, and all the declarations shouted throughout the universe, cannot subdue nor deny the emotions humans feel when someone they love goes away. Whether it's the death of a baby, a tragic accident, a divorce, or a death.

I feel like I have arrived at expressing myself and understanding my grief. I know Arthur would not have me cry the rest of my days.

"Mama, do you want a reception?"

"Oh, sorry, I was daydreaming. Yes, that will be nice for all of Arthur's friends. Hopefully, we can have the service in the middle of the afternoon." And privately, I ask God for a sunny day.

When we get home, Claire goes to the guest bedroom to pack up everything that belongs to her and Ted. I stand in the doorway watching her work. My beautiful daughter is still on a long journey through life with many heartaches probably in front of her.

But she doesn't dwell on possibilities, and I'm so glad.

I follow her out to the Buick carrying her makeup case. We put her suitcase and heavy coat in the trunk and stand there looking at one another. "I know, it's sad to say goodbye, but it's temporary."

"You're right, Mama. Why don't you drive over to my house on Saturday and I'll invite the kids to have lunch? They haven't seen you in a month. We'll talk some more about Daddy's memorial service."

"Okay, do you think Ben can put a video together about Arthur's life if I send him the pictures?" I inquire. "I'll find some snapshots of him when he was a soldier during the Korean War."

"I expect my children have never seen any of those." Claire tries to recall if she's seen them. "We'll have a good time on Saturday."

My mind is buzzing with ideas and I realize I'm a bit optimistic. I hug Claire and she gets in the car. "Be safe driving home."

"I will. The roads are clear, so I'll be just fine."

Claire turns her car around and I watch the color blue grow smaller and smaller until it disappears into the moonglow of night.

I am alone. But God is looking down. *Arthur, too.* I study the myriads of glistening stars fading through the approaching darkness.

I go back into the house and hear the landline ringing.

"Hold your horses!" I hustle through the kitchen to answer it. "Hello."

"Dorothy, it's me, Lorene."

"Lorene! Are you enjoying your visit with your daughter?"

"I'm not in Kentucky, I came home an hour ago."

"Do you have food thawed at your house?" I ask.

"No, but I can have a bowl of cereal, the milk's still good."

"Don't do that, Lorene. Come over for supper. Pack a bag and stay the night, I have a lot to tell you." I'm excited to have company.

"Okay. I was dreading staying the night alone, anyhow."

Alone. There's that dratted word again. I hate it.

"Okay then, I'm going to warm us up some supper. I have so much food leftover, delivered to my house by kind friends. Some of them go to church with me, though I don't know them very well."

"Good, I'm really hungry. I'll be over in thirty minutes."

"Perfect, Lorene. Just perfect."

I end the call and realize how lucky I am to have a *perfect* friend, a *perfect* family, a *perfect* house, and a *perfect* God who blesses me.

A Time for Caring

24

IT'S ALMOST SIX O'CLOCK when Lorene pulls her Tesla behind my old Cadillac. I hustle out on the porch to greet her with a hug.

"I've missed you so much, friend."

"I've miss you, too. Take my overnight bag while I go back to my car and get something for you." Lorene carefully steps on the flat stones Ted put down last week to avoid the mushy ground.

It's much colder outside than when Claire left for Nashville. A scant hazy moon is perched on the eastern horizon with stars out in full force bent on beautifying the universe to please their Creator.

I realize I sound awfully religious these days when I'm not cursing. Perhaps I've developed a dual personality. Satan wants part of me but God resists. I apologize to God for my bad behavior.

Lorene approaches with a small wire cage. "What do you have in there? Baby chicks?" I squint my eyes to see in the dark.

"Let's go inside and I'll show you." She's shivering.

"Here, give me the cage." I invite her to go in first and she almost stumbles over her overnight bag sitting by the door.

I remove the green vinyl covering and look at the cage good.

"Is this your new puppy, Lorene?" I inquire as she sheds her fake-fur coat and briskly rubs her hands together.

"No, the pup is yours, Dorothy. Crawford's Yorkshire Terrier gave birth to six healthy puppies in August. They're full-blooded and he planned to sell them." A tear drips down one cheek. "But I've decided to give them away as pets to my closest friends."

"Thank you, Lorene." I look at the creature and think I'll have to feed the mutt and clean up his poop. "Is this a little boy?"

"Yes, so you won't have to fool with babies coming along."

Lorene glances around my kitchen and into the den. "Everything looks exactly the same as the last time I was here."

"The only thing that's changed is Arthur no longer lives here." I don't want to think about him. "The food's warm, let's eat."

We sit down to a bowl of spaghetti with a tossed salad and glasses of cold sweet tea. Later, we'll eat the rest of the cherry pie I made for Ted with ice cream and watch a family-friendly movie.

"Have I missed anything important while I was away?" Lorene asks. "Oh, this spaghetti is the best I've had in a long time."

"Lizzy Hinson brought it over," I say.

"Did you find out if she tattled on you to Butch?"

"She says she didn't, but she's still trying to make amends." I concentrate on another subject. "I have a lot to tell you about the red mud on our guys boots, but let's finish eating first."

"Now you've really got my juices going, Dorothy."

"Well, calm them down until after supper." I say a blessing over our food and we eat quietly for a few minutes then Lorene speaks.

"Now that Crawford is gone, I need to go through our closets and pack up his things for a garage sale or give them to a charity."

"Did your sons want any of their father's things?" I ask.

"Just some tools and his guns," she replied.

"I already took care of Arthur's things. His coats and clothes are boxed at the top of the stairway. Next time Ted comes over, I'll get him to take the boxes to Good Will or the Salvation Army."

"Do you think they mind that we're discarding their *things*?"

"Lorene, that's the last thing I'm worried about," I say. "Arthur and Crawford get spotless garments to wear in Heaven. They are probably looking down at us and feeling sorry for us."

"Because our clothes aren't spotless?" Lorene tries to understand. "Mine aren't, I wash clothes every other day."

No use apologizing for a statement even I don't understand.

Silence reigns for a few seconds.

"I apologize for not inviting you to Crawford's funeral."

I see the sadness in my friend's teary gaze.

"Why didn't you call and tell me the date and time?"

"Dorothy, you were dealing with Arthur's murder so I didn't want to burden you with my grief. I hope you aren't mad I didn't."

"No, I could never be mad at you. It is what it is."

The statement is so stoic I want to puke.

"Tomorrow, I'm calling Blake Johnson at the funeral home to set a time for Arthur's memorial service. He still has the decorative urn with Arthur's ashes in it." I try to imagine how Arthur feels.

"Are you going to keep the urn here at the house?"

"I don't know, Lorene. I'm not sure what I'll do with Arthur."

The puppy begins to whine and move around in the small wire cage. "I need to take—what do you want to call him?" Lorene asks.

I think a moment. "Pepper. Just look at all that black on his furry white body." I remove him from his cage. "I'll take him out."

"Okay, you might as well start the bonding process now."

I attach a leash to Pepper's collar and he waddles behind me out the backdoor and down the porch steps. I wait for him to pee in the grass, but Pepper has to do a lot of sniffing first. Arthur's squirrel dog, Happy, died last spring from old age, so I expect Pepper has somehow picked up his scent. "Hurry up, Pepper! I'm cold."

By the time I get back in the kitchen, Lorene has finished eating. I put Pepper back into his cage and look at my spaghetti.

Red. And I'm not hungry anymore because it reminds me of mud, so I pick up our dishes and take them to the kitchen sink.

"Put your overnight bag in the guest bedroom while I load our dirty dishes in the dishwasher," I tell Lorene. "By the time you get back I'll have some Starbucks brewing and sliced pie on our plates."

* * *

"Ellie, let me in!" Butch calls out as he knocks hard on her apartment door. "Please, I need to explain." He listens through the door for sounds. "You'll be sorry if you don't talk to me."

A monster neighbor pokes his head out the door of the apartment next to Ellie's. "Is all that hollering necessary?"

"Sorry, feller, but I have to speak to my girlfriend."

The door opens. "What is it, Butch? Stop making a scene."

He doesn't care as he pushes Ellie back into the apartment, kicks the door shut with a foot, backs her up to a wall, and kisses her.

"I love you, Ellie, you can't stay mad at me."

She's wearing a housecoat and a snarly look.

"Give me two minutes to explain and I'll leave if you still want me to," he pleads for a relationship he always wanted and never had.

"Okay, but don't touch me again, you pervert!"

"I promise." Lloyd holds up his hands in defeat. "I was a senior in high school, for God's sake, Ellie. I was horny and stupid."

She slip-slides in her house shoes into the kitchen and puts on a pot of coffee. "I was half asleep and enjoying a good dream when you knocked." She refuses to look him in the eye.

"I'm sorry, Ellie, I never should've done what I did to Claire."

She turns to face him. "What gets me, Butch, is you never thought to apologize to her. Not in all these years you've known her. And she's carried this anger, like forever. You're insensitive."

Lloyd shakes his head. "I was wrong, Ellie, and I've known it for a long time. I was too embarrassed to apologize. I don't deserve a decent woman like you, but I want our relationship to last."

He bites the bullet. "Will you marry me?"

"Hell, no. I don't believe you, Butch. You've always said marriage wasn't for you. God forbid, you'd leave me at the altar like you did that bimbo, Heidi Something, over a decade ago."

The coffeemaker hisses and spits out the strong brew.

"Can we at least sit down and talk about the case?"

"You still want my help with that?"

"Yes. Can I have some of that?" He points at the coffeemaker.

"I guess." She's resigned that he's not going away yet.

Lloyd drinks his coffee black while Ellie adds cream and sugar to hers. They go into the compact den with an impressive fireplace with timbers glowing. It's only the second time he's been here, Ellie's rule. She believes a working relationship should stay just that, but they'd crossed the line, and for him there is no turning back.

He isn't sure if she feels the same way.

"I want you to take that job Sonja Berioski offered you." He savors the flavor of the coffee as caffeine impacts his bloodstream.

"I thought you said the job was dangerous."

"It is, but I spoke to Captain Colbert after Claire and her mother left the office this afternoon. She's going to have an FBI informant watch your back. If you run into trouble, he'll call her immediately."

"Who? Never mind, I know if you tell me you'll have to kill me," she teases him. "But I can tell you that doesn't make me feel all warm and fuzzy inside." She drinks from her ceramic cup.

"All we need to know is Mark Hagen's address." He listens for sounds. "Is Zoey here?" He looks in both bedrooms.

"She went back home. Her grandfather called."

"And you just let her go, Ellie?"

"Yes, she wanted to explain to Donald face to face what she's up against now that Clyde Perkins is dead," she explains.

"Well, I wish you'd phoned and told me before she left."

"Zoey will be back tomorrow night."

"I hope she'll be okay." Lloyd leans his head between his knees, so tired he feels dizzy. He'd had a couple of beers before coming here to bolster his nerve. He shakes his head and sits up.

"I want Zoey to keep working for Sonja and help you."

"You want to send a kid into the Twilight Lounge to do a man's job?" Ellie can't believe what Butch is asking of them.

Lloyd's lips wiggle. "It's the Starlight Lounge, baby."

There's fire in Ellie's emerald eyes. "Don't call me, baby. I'm not anybody's baby, and I haven't decided if I'm ever going to forgive you for what you did to poor Claire."

"Hold on, Ellie."

"And now you're using Zoey Jackson?"

"Well," Lloyd can't keep his eyes open, "if you put it like that."

"Look, if you ask Zoey to snoop for you and this FBI informant agrees to watch her back then I'm on board. But I don't want you forcing her into a compromising job that could get her killed."

"I won't, I promise." Lloyd lays his head on the back of the sofa and closes his eyes. The night disappears into thin air.

"Butch!" Ellie shakes him. "Wake up, Butch!"

But it's no use, she takes the cup from his limp hand and places it on the breakfast bar then helps him slide down on the sofa before covering him with a warm afghan. "What am I going to do with you?"

A Time to be Dutiful

25

Wednesday, November 10th

AMAZINGLY, I WAKE UP at six a.m. before my alarm clock buzzes. I want to make every moment of this day count. Then I recall I have an overnight guest. Lorene Perkins spent the night. We watched a sappy love story on the Hallmark Channel until late while pigging out on salty popcorn and diet soda. We discussed all that's happened to us this past month as if to memorialize our husbands so we can pack them away. I need to get up and make Lorene a nice breakfast.

Wearing a housecoat and slippers, I glide into the den like I'm still sixty. I'm surprised to see her sleeping in Arthur's recliner, *mine* now. Not wanting to wake her, I tiptoe into the kitchen to make the coffee.

Lorene snores loudly. She is out like a light.

While the coffeemaker does its thing, I pull the den drapes tightly over the blinds to keep out the approaching sunlight.

Feeling strangely optimistic, I tiptoe back into the kitchen and prepare my coffee with ample cream as I always do. Which reminds me of our poor old suffering cow. I need to check on Bessie.

I slip-slide into the foyer and pluck my heavy coat from the closet. Seeing none of Arthur's coats in there saddens me. But I take a deep breath and decide my life is what it is and I must press on.

Then I realize I must dress before going outdoors. And Pepper needs relief from his cage. Finally, I have it all together.

Ten minutes later, I'm on a dutiful mission. A misty darkness hovers over the morning landscape. I shine a flashlight into my pathway as I tromp in rubber boots with Pepper in my arms across the weeds to the old barn some two-hundred feet behind our house.

My house now. I'm huffing for breath by the time I reach the barn and open the door. "Bessie?" I call out to the darkness.

"Moooo!" Bessie answers me and I chuckle.

"Okay, Bessie!" I place Pepper on the ground. "Just like Arthur always did, I'll fill your bucket with fresh water and toss a bale of hay over the gate for you to munch on," I tell her, as if she understands.

"Don't die on me, Bessie!" I complete the task and find Pepper chewing on an old shoe. *Arthur's,* and it makes me feel sad.

I walk with Pepper to the other side of the barn and stare at the empty chicken cages and wish I still had fresh eggs.

But Arthur is not here to take care of them anymore.

Back at the house I find Lorene seated at the kitchen table drinking a cup of coffee. "Where were you?" she asks.

"Checking on my cow, Bessie."

Lorene yawns. "Trouble sleeping?" I inquire.

"Well, I haven't slept well since Crawford died," she tells me with grief settled in her hazel eyes. "After breakfast, I should go home."

"You want me to come with you?"

"No, I need to go alone. I might as well get used to the idea."

There's that dratted word again, *alone.*

"I suppose you'll pack up Crawford's clothes today."

"That's the plan." She sips on more coffee.

"Do you want bacon and eggs for breakfast?"

"Sure, or cereal is fine. I've been eating too much."

"I suppose people have been bringing you food like they have me for the past couple of weeks. I'm going to call Blake Johnson and set a time for Arthur's memorial service then phone Claire. She wants a reception following the service for our family and friends."

"That's nice." Lorene doesn't smile.

She's moody this morning and I feel sorry for my friend.

"Do you want to go into town and have lunch?" I ask.

She gets up from the table and stretches. "Sure."

"Good. I'll make us breakfast then you can go home and take care of your tasks. I'll pick you up at twelve fifteen, if that's okay?"

"Call first before your come."

"I will." I pause. "Lorene?"

"What?"

"You're a good friend and I love you."

"I love you too, Dorothy."

When she's ready to leave, I walk her to the car.

"See you soon," I tell her. "Call if you need me."

* * *

It's eight o'clock Wednesday morning when Ellie crawls out of bed. She looks over and sees Butch lying beside her, fully dressed, and realizes he must have abandoned the sofa something during the night and come to her bed. It's nice having him here. Maybe she will consider his proposal of marriage when the murder madness is over with and life is back to normal. Then *normal* is not a part of real life.

"Butch!" She shakes him hard. "Wake up! Go home, shower and shave, and put on some clean clothes. You have appointments this morning," she recalls. "Get up!" She shakes him again.

"Huh?" He groggily sits up. "What are you doing at my place?"

"Butch, you're at *my* apartment, don't you remember?"

"Not so much." Last night is a fog. He grabs his head.

"You drank too much, Butch."

"You have aspirin, I have a gigantic headache?" He lugs his weary body from bed and stumbles to the bathroom.

An hour later, with Butch gone, Ellie dresses for work. While driving to the office she phones Zoey Jackson's cell phone.

"Hello."

"Zoey, it's Ellie Simpson, are you okay?"

"Donald didn't come home last night. I'm worried about him."

"Does he have a girlfriend? Maybe he's at her place."

"No, work is all my grandfather knows," Zoey replies.

"Zoey, you shouldn't be alone at the house all day long. Do you have transportation?" She worries why Donald is missing.

"I can borrow Donald's motorcycle," Zoey replies.

"Come by the office and get my apartment key. You can hang out there today while I'm working," Ellie decides. "Detective Peters will find Donald for you." She adds, "Come as soon as you can."

"I will, Miss Ellie." The phone connection ends.

* * *

I am alone in my house in a rare cleaning mode. A spic-and-span house is a reflection of a clean heart and a pure soul. A gospel tape is playing on our console. It was given to me last Christmas.

I believe it was at a Sunday School party.

When I finish cleaning the guest bedroom and both bathrooms downstairs, I take a break and drink a big glass of cranberry juice. Good for the old bladder that doesn't work so well anymore.

Then I vacuum my bedroom and dust the furniture. By that time, I'm worn out and it's nearly ten o'clock. Time to phone Blake Johnson at the funeral home. I use the landline in the breakfast room and consider purchasing an iPhone from Verizon. If Crawford Perkins can learn to operate one of those fancy things, I can too.

"Oh!" I'm surprised to hear a voice answer. Then I realize I've dialed the office landline at the funeral home.

"May I help you?" Blake's secretary asks.

"Yes, this is Dorothy Powell, is Mr. Johnson there?"

"I'll transfer your call to his voicemail, he's out in the field."

I presume "out in the field" refers to a cemetery. There are two in the city and several in rural areas. "Is this Rachel?"

"Yes, it is," she replies. "If you're picking up Arthur's urn, I can handle that. All I need for you to do is sign a release paper."

When I say nothing, Rachel adds, "Then he's all yours."

I almost smile. This is a strange conversation, as if Arthur is not a person but a material possession. "No, not yet," I hear myself say.

"Okay, I'm transferring your call to Mr. Johnson's cell phone," Rachel says. "If you get his voicemail, leave your name and number and he'll call you back as soon as he can." She falls silent.

"Thank you, Rachel." I wait until voicemail clicks on.

"This is Blake Johnson, leave a message at the beep."

"This is Dorothy Powell, please call me." He has my number.

I hang up and stand idly. Blake has messed up my plans today.

However, when Lorene and I drive into town for lunch, we'll stop by the funeral home and talk to him in person.

A Time for Conclusions

26

ELLIE IS WORKING AT HER desk when Butch arrives at ten thirty.

He looks hungover and spent and the day has just started.

"You're late for work, Detective. I might fire you."

He throws a hand. "Not now, Ellie, I'm in no mood."

She resumes typing then stops. "Why not?"

"I dropped by the Captain's office this morning and she wants me to take a SWAT out to the gristmill and take a look around." He grumbles a few curse words. "Actually, two places. The old house that's an eighth of a mile from the mill." He goes into his office.

The door slams, shocking Ellie.

Being a polite responsible secretary, she knocks on the door.

"What?" Butch calls back, irritated.

Ellie is reminded this is a side of the detective that she doesn't like. Sure, he has a headache, but he's being a pain in the butt. Last night he wanted to marry her. Today, he's avoiding her.

"Is there any way I can help?" She listens through the door.

About to give up waiting and go back to her desk, the door opens and Butch comes out. He's wearing western boots and a pair of jeans with tears in the knees. The plaid shirt is lined for warmth, and he's packing a Colt .44 under the long tail of the shirt.

"Locked and loaded," Ellie teases.

"Hold my calls, I'll be back."

As he storms out of the office, Ellie calls after him, "You're not the Terminator, Butch!" She considers quitting her job.

Lunchtime, Ellie phones the oriental restaurant around the corner and orders food delivered. Someone has to watch the office.

And it appears, the privilege is all hers.

After dining on Kung Pao Chicken, Ellie phones Zoey.

"Oh, hi," the teen answers with a sharp edge to her voice.

"You never came by the office to pick up my apartment key."

"I was called into work."

"I didn't know you had a job in Columbia."

"I don't, I'm at the Starlight Lounge. Miss Sonja phoned and told me to come in, she had some office work for me."

"Zoey, I wish you'd talked to me first. How did you get to Nashville?" Ellie hoped not on Donald's motorcycle.

"Mr. Hagen picked me up at the house."

"Zoey, he's dangerous, I wish you hadn't gone."

"Donald still isn't home," Zoey says. "I don't know what's going on. I'm scared, but I have to pretend everything is okay."

"Good girl, just keep that up." Ellie recalls she hasn't yet told Butch about Donald Jackson, missing since yesterday.

"Is Mr. Hagen still at the lounge?" Ellie inquires.

"No, he dropped me off and left."

"Did he say anything of interest while you were in his car?"

"No, he just pulled in the driveway at the house and honked for me. I got in his Outback and he drove me here. I'm fine, so far."

"What kind of work are you doing, Zoey?"

"Some clerical stuff."

"See if you can get a home address for Mark Hagen."

"Okay, I'll try. Folks are pretty secretive around here."

"Be careful, Zoey. If Sonja finds out you've talked to me or Detective Peters, we cannot guarantee your safety."

Zoey's being at the dinner club feels wrong.

"I have to go now," Zoey says.

The call ends abruptly and Ellie phones Butch's cell. It goes straight to voicemail. She sighs; hands tied regarding the matter.

* * *

I pick up Lorene at twelve fifteen and we drive into town to have lunch at my favorite barbeque restaurant. Bark's Seared Pork.

Arthur and I usually ate here twice a month after church on Sundays. *Not anymore.* The owner sees me and comes over to speak.

"Oh, Dorothy, I was so sorry to hear about Arthur."

"We all are, Charlie. Thanks for asking about him." I turn to Lorene. "This is my good friend, Lorene Perkins."

She says hello then gazes around the restaurant as if there might be someone here that she knows. Then looks at Charlie.

"You have a nice restaurant, Mr. Bark."

"Thank you, Lorene." He bumps fists with her. "I hear your husband recently passed from a heart attack." He plucks two menus and personally escorts them to a table by the plate-glass window.

"Food is on the house today," Charlie tells me.

"Why, thank you, that's mighty nice of you."

"Enjoy." He's off to greet other customers.

Lorene takes a seat across the table from me. "I can see why Charlie has so many return customers. Besides serving good food, he serves friendliness." She picks up the menu to peruse her choices.

"I can't believe you and Crawford never ate here."

"He has, *had*, a finicky stomach."

I already know what I want for lunch.

"What are you ordering, Dorothy?"

"I'm having my usual, Lorene."

"Then I'll have the same." She sets her menu on the table.

"Aren't you going to ask me what I'm getting?"

"Whatever you order will be tasty," she replies.

I see tears in her eyes. "What's wrong, Lorene. Have I hurt your feelings? If you don't want barbeque, we can leave."

"No, Dorothy." She grabs my hand. "It's not that. I found my wedding scrapbook my mother put together for me and Crawford. Pictures taken in 1964 of all my family. My younger brother Anthony and his girlfriend—they looked so handsome back then."

I don't know how to comfort my friend.

She tissues her eyes. "You might recall Anthony passed away five years ago from lung cancer. He smoked a lot, you know."

I don't have sufficient words to respond.

"My grandparents were at our wedding. Do you realize I am the only one left in my immediate family? I'm seventy-six years old, and I'm the last of my breed." I know she has two sons and a daughter.

"Lorene." I reach for her hand.

"I'm sorry, I'm being a baby about Crawford's death."

"I understand viewing your wedding pictures makes you sad, Lorene. But they depict a time in your history that will become more important to your children as time passes. Your great grandchildren will see all those precious pictures and better understand their past."

I feel totally philosophical and don't recognize myself.

Lorene dries her eyes with another tissue and reaches across the table for my hand. "How did I get a friend so wise?"

Now, I want to cry. But I won't.

It's time for both of us to pack our tears away.

"What can I get you ladies?" Our waitress delivers two waters.

I order for both of us. The rest of our dining experience is better now that both Lorene and I have aired our feelings.

Somehow, I know Arthur and Crawford are proud of us.

No Time like Now

27

LLOYD USES THE GPS system on the black SUV he's driving with four trained policemen riding in the rear seats. It's a bright, sunny day so the gravel road leading to the gristmill Dorothy Powell described is navigational. "There it is, up head!" he points to it.

Lloyd pulls the truck in the muddy driveway, *red*, just like Claire and Dorothy described. Wouldn't it be ironic if the color of mud was key to solving a murder mystery, and the deceased Arthur Powell was responsible for taking down a Nashville crime syndicate?

"Okay, guys, do your thing. If there's even a scrap of paper anywhere in the mill or underneath it, I want it captured in a plastic bag for the CSI lab to process for fingerprints. Are we clear?"

"From God's mouth to ours," one of them quips.

The entire search inside and around the mill takes less than thirty minutes. Nothing. Clean as a whistle. Everyone hauls their tired butts into the truck and Lloyd drives down the road a fourth of a mile to the dilapidated house that sits on the property owned by a corporation registered in Cancun, Mexico. By now, it's 3:10 p.m.

The door to the house is open so Lloyd steps inside.

Pretty clean, he assesses, when compared to the deteriorated exterior with yellowed siding propped upon a slanted concrete slab.

He locates the bathroom first. The mirror and commode appear to be new, and the old linoleum floor has been scrubbed clean.

Hmmm. Interesting, he thinks.

"Detective, you'd better come take a look at this."

Lloyd follows Officer Cross down to the creek bed running behind the old house. He sees a floating figure, the front of the body face down in the water. "None of us touched it," Cross says.

Lloyd will. He wades into the creek in his rubberized boots and flips over the body. Donald Jackson. *Damn!* Zoey will go nuts.

"What do you want us to do with him?" Cross asks.

"Bag him and we'll drop him off at the morgue."

The process takes another fifteen minutes then they are rolling down the road toward Columbia. Nobody says anything as Lloyd listens to the wind whistle through the crevices of the doors.

In forty-five minutes, Lloyd is pulling up to the back entrance of the morgue where hospitals drop off their dead for processing.

After taking care of poor Donald, Lloyd delivers the SWAT to the main police station, turns in the police-issued truck, then drives his Blazer back to his office at Station One on Third Street.

He dreads telling Ellie about Donald Jackson. She's bonded with Zoey like a mother to a child. He rides the elevator up to the second floor and tramps into his office. Ellie is sipping on a latte.

"Did you get me one?" he asks.

"Did you get the chip off your shoulder while you were away?"

"Don't be cute, Ellie, life is not all about coffee"

"Well, it is when you wake up every morning." She trails him into his private domain and watches him strip down to his shorts.

"You gonna stand there until I'm buck naked?" he asks.

"I might, you look pretty good naked to me."

Lloyd goes into his private bathroom and slams the door. He grabs a small towel, wets it and scrubs his face and under his armpits. The clothes he'd worn to the office earlier are hanging on a hook.

He puts them on then looks in the mirror. He looks like hell warmed over twice. After wetting his hands, he threads his fingers through his long, salt-and-pepper hair. There! Best he can do.

"What? You don't have work to do?"

Ellie has her cute butt parked on the edge of his desk, her arms crossed over her ample breasts, and she's glaring at him.

"I know you found something at the mill, what?"

He walks over and pulls Ellie to her feet, puts his arms around her waist and draws her to him. "I'm so sorry, Ellie."

She pushes away and looks up at him with those huge emerald eyes. "Did you kill someone you shouldn't have?"

He takes a step back. "No, someone murdered Donald Jackson." He sees surprise tacked on her face turn to horror.

"Zoey."

"I know, I need to tell her myself. Is she at your apartment?"

Lloyd is already putting on his jacket and filling his pockets with his car keys and loose change. His billfold is stashed in the back pocket of his slacks. "Are you coming with me, Ellie?"

She has tears in her eyes. "I forgot to tell you I called Zoey. She's at the Starlight Lounge, doing some work for Sonja."

"And you just let her go?"

"No, don't blame me. She never came for my apartment key. She said Mark Hagen picked her up at Donald's house and took her to Nashville. She was afraid not to go, it might get her dead."

"Get her dead?" Lloyd shakes his head.

"Zoey's words, not mine."

"Well . . ."

"Well, what?"

He takes off his coat. "I need to think about this situation."

"Well, while you do, I have some work to do."

"Wait!" He grabs Ellie's hand. "Are we okay?"

"I guess. If you buy me supper."

"Sure. By that time, I'll have a plan."

* * *

Dorothy pulls her Cadillac under the shed's overhang and turns off the motor. "I'm glad you came home with me, Lorene. We can have supper and watch another movie tonight."

"I might want to go home after supper."

"I'll take you if you want, but you could stay another night."

"I'll think on it. Are you going to call Claire?"

"Yes, after supper. I'm hungry, are you?"

"Yes, the barbeque I ate for lunch is long gone, and our long walk in the park this afternoon tested my fortitude."

"You're not the only one." I chuckle

They get out of the car and go into the house. It's nearly dark so I switch on lights in the kitchen, breakfast room, and den.

"What do you want to eat for supper?" I look at Lorene.

"Do you have some of that delicious soup left?"

"I do." I remove the container from the fridge and pour the contents into a pot to warm the soup over the stove's gas flames.

They have peanut butter and crackers with their soup. As Lorene loads the dishwasher for me, the landline rings.

"That must be Claire." I hurry to answer the phone.

"Mama, where have you been?"

Claire sounds hysterical.

"In town, with my friend, Lorene Perkins, why?"

"Don't you ever check your phone messages?"

"I forgot to. We had a lovely lunch at Bark's Seared Pork, then took a long walk in the park. We stopped by the funeral home and I talked to Blake Johnson about Arthur's memorial service."

"Did you set a time?" Claire asks.

"Yes, next Thursday at three p.m."

"Mama, Ted and I need to spend the night with you."

"Sure, no problem." I'll need to take Lorene home. "Where are you now?" I carry the length of the phone line into my kitchen and glance out the window over the sink. I see Ted's Mercedes Benz pulling up behind my Cadillac. "Never mind, I see you now."

A few minutes later, Claire and Ted are in the kitchen with their overnight bags. "Isn't this visit kind 'a sudden?" I inquire.

"Detective Peters phoned Ted at his office an hour ago and asked him to come to his office tomorrow morning at nine o'clock. He wants to question him about the people he legally represents."

"Hello, Claire. Ted." Lorene makes her presence known.

"Good to see you again, Lorene." Ted side-hugs her.

"What did you do, Theodore?" I'm back to his formal name.

"Nothing illegal, that I'm aware of," he tells me. "Shall I put our bags in the guest bedroom?" He locks his gaze on Lorene.

"I'm not staying," she tells Theodore. "I should go home now."

"I'll drive her," Claire offers and I nod my consent.

"Sorry we didn't get to watch another movie together tonight, Lorene, but we'll get together again soon, I promise."

"Thanks for a lovely day, Dorothy."

I close the door behind them and lean against it. What is Butch looking for? Is this about bringing down the syndicate in Nashville he

146

mentioned to us the last time we were in his office? If one of the country-music artists told Ted something, he's under legal obligation not to tell another soul without that artist's permission.

Yet, something else bad has happened. *What?*"

Theodore and Claire return to the kitchen. He's shed his suit, showered, and is now wearing a pair of loose pajama bottoms with a Titan tee shirt. Claire is dressed the way she arrived, in a pair of low-cut jeans with a blousy shirt that covers the space between her waist and her butt. I've never understood how fashion came to this.

"There's enough soup left over for your supper," I tell them both. "But you're welcome to thaw steaks if you're really hungry."

"Thanks, Mama." He holds up a plastic sack from the Longhorn Restaurant. "We have takeout. Ribs with baked potatoes." He places the sack on the breakfast table.

"I'll get you some sweet tea," I offer.

"Thank you, Mama." Claire tries to smile but I can tell she's upset that Butch wants to question Theodore.

I sit at the table with them until they've finished eating.

"Ted?" I don't call him Theodore because we've moved on to a new level of family relations. "Do you know anything that will help Detective Peters find Arthur's killer and send him to prison?"

Theodore looks at Claire.

"Claire?" I'm not through with my questions. "Do you know if Ted knows something but you've promised him you won't tell me?"

I feel like I've just graduated as a trial attorney.

"Mama, he can't talk about it."

I nod. "Well, this is how it is, Theodore." I am serious as a heart attack. "You'd better tell Butch the truth! If you withhold information that will solve three murders, it won't go well with me."

"What do you mean, Dorothy?"

I note I am no longer *Mama.*

"Butch has already told me and Claire he thinks Arthur's murder is related to a crime syndicate operating out of Nashville. But he didn't tell us what sneaky business they were up to. But . . ."

I hold up my forefinger to silence any comments.

"Listen hard. If you withhold information from Butch, and I find out later, you can count me out as your mother-in-law. I will not be speaking to you, and you will not be welcome in my home."

Claire's hands cover her mouth. "You don't mean that, Mama." She looks at Ted as he glares hard at me. It's a stand-off.

I look at my daughter.

"Claire, you need to choose sides now."

"What do you mean, Mama?"

"Like Jesus once said, you're either for me or against me."

"That's harsh, Mama."

"Nevertheless," I feel unmoved by sympathy, "you support my stance, or you support your husband's. It can't be both ways."

You either serve God or serve mammon, comes to mind.

Theodore gives me one last blast of chastisement that sears right through me, spins around on his flipflops and leaves the kitchen.

"You've offended my husband!" Claire is clearly upset

"I'm not talking to you, either, until you choose sides."

I storm out of the kitchen, go to my bedroom, and slam the door *Double D-D!* I curse and hope God will forgive me.

A Time for Truth

28

Thursday, November 11th

LLOYD IS UNLOCKING THE door to his condo at 5:30 a.m. He'd spent most of last night in Nashville searching for Zoey Jackson. Before he hit the streets, he was at the Starlight Lounge. Neither Dom nor Sonja were there. John Ashbury was.

Like before, Lloyd and John had sat at the same table for two and drank beer while discussing the arrival of early winter weather and the impact the return of a nasty influenza would have on Nashville.

Lloyd had made sure Budweiser did not impair his brain.

"Where is Dom and Sonja tonight?" he'd inquired.

"Taking care of some business."

"My girlfriend Ellie told me she passed a pretty underaged girl as she and Sonja were going into the restroom last Saturday evening. Do you often hire students?" He'd pushed his luck as far as it would go.

"You're talking about Zoey. She doesn't work here any longer."

"Oh, well. I thought she might know where Sonja was. Ellie was a bit under the weather tonight. A cold coming on. But she wants to talk to Sonja about the job offer." He'd waited for input.

"Well, Lloyd, I don't know anything about that."

"Just asking." He'd snooped about all he could without bringing suspicion upon himself. "I'm looking forward to gambling soon."

"You'll have to speak to Dom. It's by invitation only."

"Sure." I tossed back my last drop of beer. "I'm going." I hang my eyes on him a bit longer. "Have Sonja call Ellie about the job."

"Will do," John says and walks away.

So, I left the lounge and spent the night driving the streets of Nashville looking for any signs of Zoey. She didn't yet know that her grandfather had been found murdered at the site of the old gristmill.

He'd wanted to tell her in person before the news media got hold of the story. Four men dead from the Columbia, Tennessee area. The killings would likely attract FOX and CNN before long.

There might even be an hour story about the murders.

Lloyd yawns. He's bone-tired. Feeling as though he's failed as a detective, he goes into his bedroom and falls prone across the bedcovers. Instantly, he sleeps. Time becomes meaningless.

His cell phone rings and it wakes him.

"Ellie, what's up?"

"Where are you, Detective Peters?"

He knows there's someone with her in the office.

"What time is it?"

"Nine fifteen. Attorney Theodore Burkes is here. He says he has an appointment with you at nine. That was fifteen minutes ago."

"Tell Mr. Burkes I'm on my way."

A one-minute shave, a three-minute shower, dressing in less than four minutes, Lloyd is out the door and on his way to the office.

* * *

Claire Burkes' husband looks as disgruntled as Lloyd feels. He has no idea where Zoey Jackson is, or why someone murdered her grandfather. Is the Mafia getting rid of anyone who knows anything about their lucrative prostitute business? In that case . . .

"Theodore Burkes." Ted introduces himself.

"Good to meet you." Lloyd ignores the fist-bump. "Ellie hold my calls." He looks at the attorney. "Let's talk in my office."

Lloyd is discombobulated, his thoughts so scattered he doesn't know if he has the ability to adequately question the lawyer that represents several high-profile and wealthy country-music stars.

Ellie has made coffee and the carafe sits on a small table underneath the window of Lloyd's compact office.

"I need caffeine, you?" Lloyd asks Theodore.

Ted waves him off. "No, what's this meeting about?"

Lloyd takes in a huge breath of oxygen and gulps down a few sips of coffee to clear the fog out of his stunned brain.

"Have a seat, Attorney Burkes."

"I have an eleven o'clock appointment in Nashville this morning, so let's get the questions over with so I can leave."

Lloyd can see Theodore is operating on a short fuse. He wonders how solid his relationship is with Claire. If he had a mother-in-law as irritating as Dorothy Powell, he'd be operating on a short fuse, too. Lloyd scratches his itchy scalp, having skipped washing his hair while showering this morning.

Time to wake up and do his job.

"Have you heard of a prostitute ring operating in Nashville?"

"Everyone knows one exists," Ted replies. "Four major highways cross through the city. Love is popular with tourists."

It irritates Lloyd that prostitution is compared to love.

"Have any of your music clients specifically mentioned names associated with the organizers of a prostitute ring?"

"What my clients tell me is confidential," Ted says, recalling Dorothy's ultimatum. "But there is someone you can talk to."

"Who?" Lloyd removes a pen and notepad from the top drawer of his desk. "Be specific and give me a phone number if you have one." He waits for the information, feeling time is not wasted.

* * *

I have been up since five a.m. reading my Bible. I know I was hard on Theodore last night, but I feel he will tell Butch whatever he knows about the crime syndicate operating in Nashville.

I'm sweeping the back porch when Claire comes out and sits in the swing holding Pepper. He's content as a knot on a log.

"Mama, Ted will do as you asked, so don't stay mad."

"I'm not, Claire." I sweep hard. I'm mad at myself for putting a wedge between me and my only living child.

"He's going to text me when he finishes talking to Butch."

I sweep the mud and grit out the porch door then off the steps with the broom. "I'm not mad, Claire. Just upset that it's taking this long to identify Arthur's killer. Lorene feels the same way."

Claire sets the swing to rocking. The weather is warmer today, in the low sixties, but it won't last long. A northern front is predicted to blow in my late tomorrow. A blast of cold, possibly some snow.

"When Ted comes back, we're heading home."

I nod, no verbal response.

"Do you want to talk about the reception following Daddy's memorial service next week?" Claire asks.

"You plan it, I have enough to think about." I prop my broom against the screen door and sit in the swing with Claire.

"After we bury Daddy, are you going to live here alone?"

Alone. I wish Webster had never printed that word.

"I don't know. I'm going to get Jacob Dunwoody to help me cancel everything in Arthur's name then I'll decide if I want to sell the house." I roll my shoulders. "It's a lot to think about."

"Yes, it is, Mama. And I'll be glad to help you anyway I can."

I wrap an arm around Claire's waist. "I know, and if Jacob and I can't figure out things, I'll certainly call on you and Ted."

I'm back to calling my son-in-law Ted, because I trust he will do the right thing. Claire's cell phone rings. She looks at me.

"It's Ted. I need to take this." She walks out into the yard.

I watch her sullen expression turn into one of surprise, maybe joy. She ends the calls and comes up the steps to the porch.

"Ted gave Butch the name of someone who knows young girls willing testify in court concerning a Mafia-operated prostitute ring."

"Are you saying this crime syndicate Butch talks about is run by thugs preying on young girls, compelling them to prostitute their bodies for pay?" I don't like to think things like that exist.

"Yes. I'm going to get our bags packed."

Claire goes into the house and I follow her. "Did Ted say anything about me?" I hope he's not still furious with me.

"No, but he'll be okay, give him some time."

"Will you take care of the details regarding the service and reception next week?" I ask as she walks into the den.

Claire turns around. "Sure. You want your minister to preach a short sermon?" she inquires. I nod that I do. "Okay then."

Ted returns to the house around ten o'clock and he drives off with Claire fifteen minutes later. I watch them and wave as they go.

Then I go back in the house and sit in the den. I don't know how to spend the rest of the day. But I need to figure out how to be alone.

A Time to Forgive

29

Friday, November 12th

LATE YESTERDAY, LLOYD HAD met with Anthony Ricardo on the outskirts of Nashville. Tony was an upcoming country-rap star. He especially appealed to young teens who liked to dance. And he was move-star quality with his Latino good looks and perfect physique.

Theodore Burkes had called Tony and set up the meeting. Lloyd recalled their conversation while seated at a park in Green Hills.

"I don't like Mafia guys preying on young Spanish girls," Tony said right off. "For the most part, they've come to America illegally to work and make a better life for themselves. Like me."

"I need solid witnesses to make arrests," Lloyd had told him.

"I can give you the names of four girls who were forced into prostitution by a woman who calls herself Sonja."

Lloyd smiled. "We've met."

Tony nodded. "Drop-dead gorgeous."

"Have you heard of a girl named Zoey Jackson?"

"Yeah, Maria told me a cou'pla days ago a girl named Zoey was scheduled to be shipped to Columbia then sold to a wealthy sheik in the Middle East," Tony had revealed. "You know her?"

"Yeah, she's from my hometown."

"That's all I know about it."

"Here's my email address. Send me the names and numbers of the girls willing to testify against Sonja and her boss, Dom."

"Are we done here?" Tony asked.

"Yeah, and congratulations on your big success."

"Only in America," Tony had said, then walked away.

Lloyd had rested well last night, feeling on the precipice of solving four crimes and taking down a crime syndicate in the process.

Captain Colbert had spoken to the State Director of the FBI and given him the names of the four Latina girls willing to testify in court against Sonja Berioski and Dom, the Somalian with no last name.

It was out of Lloyd's purview now, but he owed Dorothy Powell a promised phone call. He couldn't tell her everything he'd found out but enough to satisfy her curiosity. He dialed her landline.

"Hello," she answers.

"This is Detective Peters," he tells her.

"Yes, Butch?"

He considers hanging up and breaking his promise.

"Dorothy, I promised to call you if I had new information."

"Yes, you did, Detective Peters." *I am nicer now.*

"The people we believe are responsible for murdering your husband, Crawford Perkins, and Clyde Willems', are going to be arrested by the FBI before today is over." He's fulfilled his duty.

"Well, that's great news, Detective Peters."

"I know you're still peeved at me for feeling Claire up and down when I was a senior in high school. I'm better than that now. I'm asking for your forgiveness. I don't want to dislike you anymore."

I swallow hard and process Butch's apology.

"How can I not forgive you, Lloyd? You've been honest with me and I appreciate it. I know Arthur will ask God for Brownie points to be put beside your name in Heaven. Thank you."

Lloyd chuckles. "I don't know about Brownie points, but it feels good to be on solid ground with you again. When is Arthur's memorial service?" He grabs a pen and notepad.

"Next Thursday, at three p.m. I hope you can make it. And bring Ellie. She's classy and will pull you up to her standard."

"I don't know if that's a compliment or not."

"Don't pay any attention to me, I'm an old woman."

"Don't be a stranger, Dorothy," Lloyd says.

"Come out to the house for coffee, or better, lunch. I have no intention of walking into a police station or a detective's office for the rest of my life." *Which may not be all that long, I think.*

Why am I beating up on myself?

I dial Lorene's phone number?

"Hello?"

"Lorene, can I come over for a visit?" I ask.

"Sure. Do you want to have lunch with me?"

"That sounds good, see you in a few."

I go into my bedroom and exchange my pajamas for a pair of jeans and a warm flannel shirt. Before I leave that end of the house, I check the guest bedroom to make sure Claire and Ted have not left clothes items or toiletries. Then I gather the dirty towels in the hall bath.

Turning out the lights as I walk toward the kitchen, I set my big purse on the kitchen cabinet and look out the window at the backyard. I imagine that I see Arthur walking around and that he looks at me.

"Hi, darling. I miss you. I'll come for a visit soon."

After I let Pepper out to pee and lock him in his cage, I leave the house in my old Cadillac and vow to get a brand-new vehicle of some kind as soon as I receive the payout from Arthur's life-insurance policy.

Then I'm on my way driving to Lorene's house for a visit.

She waits on the front porch for me, waving at a distance. I thank God for a good friend that lives close. Someone that I can call and drop in on at any time of the day. We are bosom buddies.

"I was going to call you if you hadn't called me," Lorene says right off. "I saw in the newspaper that the high school janitor turned up dead in Rutherford County not far from Murfreesboro."

We go inside her house because a brisk cold wind has come up.

"Want a cup of coffee?" Lorene asks.

"Sure. Where was the janitor found?" I sit at her breakfast bar.

"Floating in a creek behind an old gristmill," she answers.

Now, that is news Butch didn't tell me.

"Lorene, this is the same location where Crawford and Arthur picked up red mud on the soles of their boots," I remind her.

She's sullen over the idea.

"Good news," I say, "Butch phoned me before I called you and said the FBI plans to make arrests later today. He was talking about the people that killed your husband, mine, and Clyde Willems."

"And now, we can add a janitor to their murderous acts," Lorene concludes. "So, someone scared my Crawford to death."

"Threats likely, but they didn't touch him," I say.

"Well, he might've had a heart attack anyway, we'll never know for sure." Lorene would like to think his death was of natural causes.

She fixes our coffees and brings them to the bar. "Dorothy? I think it's time we put all this tragedy behind us and live our lives."

"I hope we can." I keep thinking that another shoe will drop like Cinderella's and the bad sisters will dominate my life.

"What do you want to do before lunch?" she asks.

I shrug. "Can I help you with anything?"

"I was thinking of going up in the attic and packing up stuff I'll never need again. You feel like climbing up with me?"

"Are you talking about getting on one of those rickety ladders you pull down from the ceiling?" I ask to clarify.

"No, I guess you've never been upstairs. In the hallway on the second level, Crawford had our builder install a set of stairs going up to the attic. It's completely safe. He knew we'd get old."

"Okay, I'm game then."

* * *

Ellie comes into the office later than usual. Lloyd's office door is open and he hears her come in. She plops her purse on the desk where the computer rests, then enters the compact kitchen.

Lloyd follows her to the door. "You wonder where I was last night?" He sees her shoulders tighten from the back.

"I'm sorry I didn't call you but my phone battery crashed."

She fills the coffeemaker with water and Folgers and watches as it brews the coffee. She doesn't turn around. She's really mad.

"The FBI made the arrests last night."

Ellie turns around, her emerald eyes the size of moonrocks.

"You know who killed Arthur Powell?"

"Claire Burkes' attorney husband, Theodore, gave me the name of an upcoming country-western singer, so I set up a meeting."

There are tears in Ellie's eyes. "Butch, why didn't you tell me?"

"Too dangerous, I didn't want you involved."

"Don't you trust me?"

"I trust myself to get the job done," he says.

"Did you find Zoey?"

"No, I think she's on her way to Columbia to be sold to a sheik in the Middle East." Lloyd comes clean about the teen.

"Does she know Donald was murdered?"

"Ellie, you've done nothing but ask questions since I came into the kitchen. I have one for you. Will you marry me? I'm serious."

She turns around and fixes herself a cup of coffee.

"Ellie? You don't have to answer today. Think about it."

She turns around, her eyes bright with an idea.

"Let's go get Zoey?"

"What?"

"Let's tell the FBI to go and get our girl," Ellie explains. "She's a material witness and can testify in court that she gave Mark Hagen the names of young girls that wanted to work in prostitution. You've already basically promised her immunity if she testifies. Right?"

"I said I wouldn't arrest Zoey. I can't vouch for the FBI."

"Talk to Captain Colbert. Tell her how Zoey gave you leads that helped solve these local murders. I want her back, Butch."

"Okay, Ellie." He thinks on it. "Okay, I'll give it a try."

A Time to Beware

30

I AM BACK HOME FROM Lorene's by three o'clock. Thursday has already been too long a day despite Daylight Saving time. I helped Lorene pack up Crawford's hunting clothes and stuff he'd never use again. We drove into Columbia and dropped the boxes off at the Help Center. Now, I am sitting here in my den, feeling lonely.

I am about to turn on the TV when I hear my front door chimes go off. "Who in the world?" I ask myself as I trot down the hall leading to the front foyer. I peek out the side-glass panel.

There's a handsome man standing on my front porch. He's wearing a dark suit and carrying a large bouquet of red roses.

I unlock the door and peek through a crack. "Did I win the Sweepstakes?" I had ordered magazines last month to enter.

"Open the door, Mrs. Powell. These are for you."

I feel safe so I open the door. "Who are you?"

His smile is beautiful. "You don't know me but I knew Arthur." He hands me the bouquet. "You should put these in water."

"Of course," I say back.

"I could use a drink of water myself. May I come with you?"

"Certainly. Call me Dorothy, please. I am so delighted to have company. It seems God has smiled down on me this afternoon."

"Yes, God acts in strange ways," he comments as he trails me down the long hall into the breakfast room. He stands there as I fix him a glass of cold refrigerator-filtered water and give it to him.

"Thank you, this is very kind of you, Dorothy."

"Why don't we sit in the den and you can tell me how you knew my Arthur." I turn up my palm to gesture him to enter first.

My husband's friend, or acquaintance, sits down on the sofa.

"You have a nice restful place, Dorothy." He glances around the room. "Do you live alone? Any children staying with you now?"

"My daughter Claire stayed with me last week. I was in House Arrest, so I couldn't stray farther than fifty feet in any direction."

"Well, it seems you're a free woman now."

"Yes, I am, and it truly feels good." I look at him hard. I don't know this stranger's name yet, and I'm a bit nervous he's here.

"How do you know my Arthur?" I inquire as I rock in my recliner and drink from a glass of water. "You know he passed."

"Yes, I knew that." He finishes his water and sets it on the side table. "We only met once, but it was quite memorable."

"How so, Mr. . . .?"

"Mark. Mark Hagen."

"Mr. Hagen, tell me about your one encounter with Arthur."

"Well, Dorothy, he took something from me that was important." Mark's gaze becomes less than friendly. "So, I took from him something more important." He wickedly grins. "I still am."

"I don't understand, Mark. What are you taking from Arthur?"

He smiles. "You, Dorothy. *You.*"

I feel in my bones this conversation is all wrong.

"Who are you, Mark? And who do you work for?"

"I work for some powerfully wealthy people," he tells me. "I don't even know their names because there are layers upon layers of secrets. Many, many go-betweens before instructions get to me."

"What do you do for these wealthy layered people?" I ask.

"I'm a hitman." He grins. "Do you know what that is?"

"You kill people?"

"Yes, Arthur was the last person I talked to before I talked to Crawford Perkins, also the last person he talked to."

His sentences were multilayered too, but I got the gist of it.

"Are you going to kill me, Mark?"

He grins. "Figure it out. I wanted to meet the woman that's been causing a lot of trouble for me and my friends."

* * *

It's past eight p.m. and Claire has been trying to call her mother since dark. At last resort, she dials Lloyd Peters' cell number.

"Butch, this is Claire. Have you spoken to my mother today?"

"Yes, in fact I phoned her with an update regarding your daddy's case. I also apologized for feeling you up and down when I was young and stupid. Did she tell you that? Is that why you're calling."

"No, but I forgive you. I can't get ahold of Mama. I'm worried something bad has happened to her. Do you mind driving out to her house and checking on her for me? The key is under the potted plant at the backdoor of the porch. I would really appreciate it."

"No problem. I'm at Ellie's apartment. She can go with me."

"Thanks, Butch. Call me when you get to the house."

"Was that Claire on the phone?" Ellie asks.

"Yes, she's wants me to drive out to Dorothy's house and check on her. She's not answering her phone. Want to come with me?"

"Sure, have you called Lorene Perkins? She might be there."

"Good idea," Butch answers. "I'll do that right now."

He has both women saved in his Contact List.

The phone rings a couple of times before she answers.

"Mrs. Perkins, this is Detective Peters." He waits while she thanks him for his efforts in helping solve Arthur Powell's murder.

"No thanks necessary, Mrs. Perkins. Is Mrs. Powell with you?"

"No, Dorothy went home middle of the afternoon."

He waits while Lorene explains how they had gone up the stairs to the attic and loaded up all of Crawford's hunting clothes and paraphernalia then taken them to Colombia to give to Good Will.

"Did you try her at her house?" Lorene asks.

"No, but Claire did and she isn't answering the landline."

"Do you want me to drive over and check on her?"

Butch grins. "Do you mind, then call me?"

"Sure, no problem. I'm on my way now."

He ends the call and looks at Ellie. "It might save us a trip out to the house." But his fiancée isn't smiling.

"What?" The woman has a mind of her own.

"Claire asked *you* personally to check on Dorothy."

"I know. But I learned a long time ago that it saves time if you designate responsibilities to others." He smiles at his cleverness.

"I think we should go and see for ourselves if she's fine."

"Not yet."

"Okay, you stay here and keep the fire going. I'm putting on my coat and driving out to the house to check on Dorothy."

"Okay, Ellie, I surrender." Butch is reminded that this is the very reason he opposes marriage. "I'm coming with you."

A Time to Meet the Wizard

31

LORENE FINDS THE KEY to the back porch under a pot of dead Peonies and lets herself inside the house. No lights are on.

"Dorothy!" She calls out loudly. "Are you here?"

No answer comes forth as Lorene turns on the kitchen lights and ventures into the den. Everything looks in order. She proceeds through the den and down the hall to the master bedroom.

Dorothy's bed is made and nothing looks disturbed.

Where are you friend? She questions.

She returns to the kitchen and dials Detective Peter's cell phone number. He answers on the first ring.

"Dorothy isn't here," she says first off.

"Thank you, Ms. Perkins, Ellie and I are on our way there."

"Shall I wait for you before I go home?"

"I think that would be best. You may have been the last person to see Dorothy today," he says. "Maybe another friend came and got her. Maybe she is at a movie in town and having a good time."

"No, Dorothy would've told me if she was going somewhere," Lorene insists. "We watch each other's backs, especially now that a murderer is still out there somewhere walking free."

"I understand. Why don't you lock the doors and we'll knock on the front door when we get there? Okay?"

"Sure. That's a good idea."

The house feels creepy, like it has secrets hiding in its old walls. Locked inside should make Lorene feel better but it doesn't. She feels Arthur's ghost walking around, also looking for Dorothy.

It sends shivers down her spine.

Lorene turns on the television and sits on the sofa while waiting. The den clock says 9:02 p.m. and she realizes how tired she is.

Another fifteen minutes goes by before she hears the door chimes go off. Detective Peters and Ellie have arrived.

Trotting down the hall to the foyer, she peeps through the sidelights first. It's them. She unlocks the door and opens it.

"I'm so worried about Dorothy, this isn't like her," Lorene tells them as they enter the foyer. "Something bad has happened."

"Now, Lorene." Ellie gives her a light hug. "Don't you worry, we'll find Dorothy soon. Let's not assume the worst."

"The worst? Like she's already dead?"

"No, Ms. Perkins, Dorothy is fine," Lloyd says. "May we come in and have a look around the house. Maybe she left a note."

"No note," Lorene says, "I already looked."

Ellie holds Lorene's cold hands. "We're here now, so relax."

"Thank you, Ellie, you have a kind heart." She gives Butch a hard look, and he knows she doesn't feel the same way about him.

"We need to take a look around, Lorene." Ellie walks towards the back of the house as Lorene trails a step behind.

"I'm going to check out back," Lloyd tells the ladies.

The back door shuts with a bang.

The women carefully check both the master bedroom and the guest bedroom for clues. Everything seems in order. Five minutes later, Lloyd comes inside as Ellie and Lorene return to the kitchen.

"What's that thing in your palm?" Lorene asks Lloyd.

"Something I found it in a bush by the porch stairs," he replies.

Ellie spies the speck of red in his hand. "What is it?"

"Not sure." Lloyd smells it. "Fresh and velvety soft." He wonders if a delivery man was here. But where are the roses?

"Did you search the house, Ellie?" he inquires.

"Nothing is out of order," Lorene answers for them both.

Lloyd stands in the kitchen and wonders if the person who delivered the roses is not who he said he was. The Mafia has been systematically eliminating everybody associated with Arthur's death.

Maybe, someone came after Dorothy because she's caused so much grief. "What are you thinking, Butch?" Ellie asks.

"That Dorothy may have been abducted."

"Oh, my Lord!" Lorene loses it and becomes hysterical. "Do you think whoever killed Arthur and Crawford took her?"

"I know where she is," Ellie says with clarity.

"You do?" Lloyd and Lorene simultaneously respond. "Where do you think she is, Ellie?" he asks his secretary-turned detective.

"The old gristmill, where they found Donald Jackson's body floating in the creek. Let's go get our woman!"

Butch inwardly smiles. Ellie has really finetuned her detective instincts. "Can I go with you?" Lorene asks.

"No," Lloyd answers. "We'll follow you back to the house. You can lock up before we leave. We promise to call you when me find Dorothy." *If we find her*, Butch worries she's already dead.

* * *

I am blindfolded. Mark Hagen has stuffed me in the backseat of his Outback and driven for a long distance, I think for over an hour.

I'm cold in the backseat since the heat comes out under it. Arthur's killer didn't give me time to fetch my coat before he dragged me out of my house like a madman. Pepper probably needs to pee by now. I'm as pissed-off as a rooster in a cockfight. But I will show no fear. I won't give him that. The vehicle is slowing down.

Where are we? The car engine grows quiet as I lay down in the backseat, my hands and legs bound with packing tape. I hear my abductor get out of the car then the backdoor opens. The air is cold as he rips the tape off my ankles and drags me out of the vehicle.

Still blindfolded, I am shoved up a couple of steps and stumble on the last one as I hear him kick open a door.

"Move forward, Dorothy," he says then pushes me.

"Thank you, Mister Killer, that is so kind of you."

He sneers. "Sarcasm won't save your life, Mrs. Powell."

"I'm not worried, the likes of you will be in Hell soon."

He snatches the blindfold off my eyes.

"What's next?" I'm back at the old gristmill Claire and I drove past last week. "Can't you get any more creative than this?"

"What do you mean?" His lizard-colored eyes narrow with interest. "You've been here before?" He appears surprised.

"Drove past," I reveal, the day the blizzard struck.

He nods. "How did you find our hiding place?"

"First, tell me what you've been hiding."

"Young girls, prostitutes about to go to work for us," he replies.

That is something new under the sun, something that Butch had not told me. "Lorene Perkins found this address in the Contact List of Crawford's iPhone," I tell him, thinking the more I keep him interested in what I'm saying the more time I have left to live.

"Tell me about the red mud." His lips wiggle with amusement.

"First clue!" I exclaim with pride. "Our husbands brought the red stuff home on their boots and ruined our rugs."

"Yours and Mrs. Perkins."

I nod. "Later, my daughter Claire found a pair of boots owned by Clyde Willems' in the bedroom closet of his old log cabin. That's where Claire bumped into Sonja." I am so on fire with the truth.

Mark curses. "I hate loose ends."

"That's okay, feller, if you ask God to forgive you, He will. And go ahead and confess to murder while you're at it," I tell him.

"You're not afraid of me, or dying, are you?"

"Nope." My chin is set hard and I'm super focused on him.

"You should be, you're just an old woman."

"Wrong again. I'm not old until the best part of my day is going to bed at night. And if you kill me, I promise to be looking down from Heaven while the fires of Hell get hotter because of it."

Mark's expression is one of surprise. Then he reaches around his back and comes out with a Smith-and-Wesson 9mm that was jammed in his belt. "Time to shut you up, old woman!"

I say a few Hail Mary's in the name of Jesus, God is great and God is good, close my eyes, and wait to see Arthur on the other side.

Then I hear a phone ring. I open one eye.

"Yeah, she's here with me."

Mark looks at me while he listens.

"If you say so." He slams the phone shut. "You're a damn lucky woman, Dorothy! Let's take a ride."

"Oh, goody! Am I gonna git to meet the big boss?"

* * *

Lloyd doesn't need GPS to find the gristmill in Rutherford County. Ellie is convinced her abductor has taken Dorothy there.

It's after eleven p.m. when he parks in front of the old gristmill.

"Ellie, stay in the car," he instructs her then gets out and spies Claire Burkes standing in the yard, glaring through the dark.

"Ellie called, so I came to meet you," Claire says. "There were fresh tire tracks when I got here. I may have messed them up."

By this time, Ellie is out of the truck and has joined them.

They walk around the side of the gristmill to the back, using a flashlight to keep from tripping over fallen branches. The moon shines brightly so the creek behind the mill is clearly visible.

"At least, Mama's not in there," Claire notes.

"Yeah." Lloyd grunts, relieved. "Let's take a look inside the mill then see what's breathing at the old house down the road."

Claire nods. They find nothing of interest in the mill.

Then Butch bends over and picks up a tiny fleck of red. He grins. Dorothy Powell has a real sense of humor. *Red.*

He hands the speck to Claire. It's velvety soft and red.

"It's a piece of a rose petal," she tells Butch.

"Dorothy's abductor brought her a bouquet of fresh red roses," Lloyd concludes. "That's how he got inside the house."

Claire says, "He brought Mama a peace offering."

"But I saw no roses at the house," Ellie recalls.

"Easy, he takes the bouquet with them," Lloyd concludes.

They get back in the truck. "But Dorothy managed to pinch off a few petals. She's dropping them as clues, so we can follow them."

"I always knew Mama had a detective's heart," Claire says.

"Where do we go next?" Ellie inquires.

"I don't know. Maybe Clever Dorothy will call us."

A Time to Wage War

32

"I KNOW YOU'RE A HARDENED criminal, Mr. Hagen." Since I know his name and what he's done, I may not live long enough to tell anyone.

"Well," he shrugs, "I'm glad you understand that, Dorothy."

I'm not through yet. "Mr. Hagen, even people condemned to the guillotine get a last request. A favor before death consumes them."

I'm feeling rather optimistic despite my dire circumstances. Arthur is watching over me, I'm convinced. And God is good.

"Don't I get a last request before you execute me?" I inquire.

I recall a scene Arthur and I watched on television. One of those prison-type 1960s flicks. I wait for his decision, my life on the line.

"Okay, what is your request, Dorothy?"

"Do you mind stopping at a drive-through restaurant and getting us a hot cup of coffee? I'm freezing my buns off."

I glare at him, praying to Jesus he'll take the bait.

"You're a piece of work, Mrs. Powell."

"I know what that means, I'm not stupid. Thank you."

"Well, so happens I want a cup of Joe, too." He rolls off the next exit and pulls in the line to a McDonald's take-out console.

We wait ten minutes before our turn to order. *Oh goody*! I've delayed my execution but I need to do more than just delay.

The teen at the take-out window passes two Styrofoam cups of coffee with lids to Mr. Hagen. The customer behind honks for us to get out of the way, so he sets our coffees in cupholders between us. My hands are no longer bound since I'm about to have the last treat of my life. "Here. Let me open yours." I grab his cup of coffee.

I pretend to spill some of his as I lift the lid.

"Sorry, I need to get a tissue from my purse to clean up the mess," I tell him then bend over as if it's the most natural thing I've ever done. While I'm reaching in my purse, I uncap my bottle of sleeping pills and grab several with my free hand. As I sit up, I drop them in his cup.

"There!" I swipe the liquid off the console as he enters the flow of traffic and swings on to the interstate, I presume to Nashville.

When we were cruising at a legitimate speed down the highway, he reaches for his cup and takes a sip. "Hell, it's bitter as gall."

"Mine, too," I say, "but at least it will keep us warm and alert."

"Yeah." He gulps down the coffee like he's thirsty.

I restrain from wailing like at wolf at the moonlit night. I wish Arthur could be here to see how clever I've been. Maybe God will tell him I'm getting even with his killer. It should put a smile on his face.

I feel the car slowing down. "Hey, are you okay?"

"A little woozy, guess I've been up too long today."

His next statement is garbled and the car is swerving along the interstate like it's drunk. "Pull over to the side of the highway."

But he isn't answering. He's passed out.

Oh, brother, I wonder how many sleeping pills I put in his coffee cup. The car swaggers like a drunken soldier. I have to do something.

I pull up the console between us and give his limp body a shove against the door. My left foot clumsily finds the brake pedal and I pump it gently. the Outback slows down enough for me to pull over to the side of the interstate. I kill the motor and hope I didn't kill Mr. Hagen. Terrified, yet rewarded, I sit there for a while.

"Well, that was certainly interesting. Something new under the sun." I'm convinced the rest of my life will be full of surprises.

* * *

Claire answers her cell phone. "Who is this?"

"Your mother," I reply.

"Why are you calling on someone else's phone. We were worried sick about you. Are you okay? Were you abducted?"

"Claire. Shut up and listen for once!" I am the commander of my future now that my abductor is lost in Wonderland.

"Dorothy, this is Detective Peters."

"Are you having an affair with my daughter?"

"He isn't," I hear Ellie say and feel some better.

"Where are you, Dorothy?" Butch asks. "We found the rose petal you dropped at the site of the old gristmill. We figured out that was where your abductor took you. Where is he now?"

"I'm sitting in Mark Hagen's Outback," I tell Butch. "He's sleeping off a handful of my sleeping pills I put in his cup of coffee."

"It's me, Mama. Are you crazy? You could've been killed!"

"He was gonna to kill me with his gun, but got a call from someone higher up that changed his mind."

I think God works in mysterious ways.

"Mama, do you know how lucky you are?"

"Lucky? Did you forget I have skills?"

I hear laughter, my daughter and Butch have no faith in me.

"I'm sitting on Interstate 40 at Exit 20, can you come get me?"

"On our way, Mama. But don't hang up."

"I won't, but hurry, Mr. Hagen might wake up and I'd have to hit him in the head with the butt of his super-duper killer gun."

I know Claire's phone is on an open channel.

"Butch might arrest me for that," I tease him.

"Cute, Dorothy, sit tight we're on our way," he says.

A Time to Remember

33

Thursday, November 18ᵗʰ

IT'S A WEEK BEFORE Thanksgiving and I am wearing the pretty pink suit Arthur gave me two Christmases ago. The organ music siphoning through the speakers is playing *I Come to the Garden Alone*.

And I know Arthur has already taken that walk.

Family and friends have gathered in one of the largest reception rooms available at Johnson's Funeral Home. Many have already greeted me and taken their seats in preparation to memorialize my husband, Arthur Daniel Powell. Claire sits on one side, Ted on the other. Lorene Perkins is in the seat directly behind me, patting my shoulder ever so often and softly sniffing as she grieves for me.

I am so fortunate to have such a good friend.

As I watch Arthur's life unfold on a video my grandson Benjamin prepared, I see clips of him from the time he was a baby till he passed at the age of eighty-two on Monday, October 25ᵗʰ.

I meditate on our time together as husband and wife. Patrick Swayze had it right when he told Demi Moore that you take the love with you. I know Arthur's affection is as everlasting as mine is.

I turn around in my seat to see how many people have come to honor Arthur. Butch, Ellie, and a young girl I don't recognize are coming through the door at the back. I wonder what story the girl holds and how much more Detective Peters is keeping to himself.

Brother Kenny from the First Methodist Church approaches me.

"How are you holding up, Dorothy?" he inquires.

"I'm fine, thank you." In fact, I'm *perfect* because Arthur's killer and his crime-syndicate buddies are all behind bars.

"I think everyone who's coming has been seated," my pastor whispers. "We'll begin the service now, if you're ready."

"I'm ready." Trust me, I'm so ready to take Arthur's urn home with me and scatter his ashes over the cow pasture. I know that's where he'd want to rest until Jesus returns and gives him a new Heavenly body. We'll probably both get one together.

It's a nice sermon intended to bring comfort to all who listen. To all who have suffered loss, and to all who will in the future. There're two things that are certain, Arthur always said.

Death and Taxes. And now I know memories are certain, too.

As the service draws to a close, Claire gets up and steps upon the stage decorated with beautiful flower arrangements. She reads a eulogy, a poem she has written to her daddy for this special occasion.

Then Theodore has a word or two to say.

Helen and Benjamin come next.

Those are all nice words but they won't bring Arthur back to me.

No, I must go to him if we are ever to be together again.

"Dorothy?"

I dry my tears and look up. "Yes, Brother Kenny?"

"Would you like to come up on the stage with me and say something about Arthur?" I nod and dry my tears with a tissue.

I stand on the stage alone, gazing down at my sweet family. Then I look at our friends, so many I can't count. They've all come to say goodbye to Arthur. I am overcome with love for them all.

"Dorothy?"

I realize I'm taking too long. I clear my throat.

"Arthur was a good husband. I will miss him."

A Time to Gather

34

Thursday, November 25ᵗʰ

A WEEK AGO, I SAID goodbye to Arthur in front of my family and friends. Today, my family gathers around my dining-room table for a noon Thanksgiving dinner. I sit at one end of the oblong table while Arthur's urn occupies the captain's chair at the other end.

To my right is my daughter, Claire. Between her and husband Ted sits Little Billy, my four-year-old great grandson. His younger sister June, nearly three, sits across from him between their parents, Helen and Patrick. If Benjamin gets marries and has children, I'll need to keep a calendar of all their names and birthdates.

I'm still young, but I'm wearing out. I know my time is coming to take a walk across that great expanse where timeless joy will greet me in the Afterlife. Hopefully, Arthur is there. Now, I'm being silly.

And I suppose I'll never know why Arthur and Crawford lent Clyde Perkins money. Maybe Clyde wanted to do the right thing by paying off a debt and seeking a better life. There are things Detective Butch knows that he'll never tell me. And that's okay. I'm okay.

I stand up and ring the old-fashioned dinner bell as Arthur always did, as his father did, and his grandfather. It's a tradition in the Powell family to ring in the gathering of family members.

"Thank all of you for coming," I say with a smile. I look to the end of the table. "You, too, Arthur." And that brings chuckles.

"I'm not being disrespectful of the dead," I explain my former comment, "but we all know Arthur is not in that urn. What's left of his worn-out body has been turned into ashes. But it's not him."

"Amen!" Benjamin lifts his water glass, and I think he might turn out to be a preacher like my daddy. "To Granddaddy!"

"To Granddaddy!" We all lift our glasses to toast him.

"Ted, will you say the blessing over our food." I sit down.

"Yes, Mama, I'll be glad to."

I listen as he reads a prayer from one of the Catholic Saints, and know he's Baptist, and wonder why he isn't quoting Billy Graham.

"Ben, do us the honor of serving the turkey," I say.

At Claire's insistence, I ordered the turkey and dressing from Kroger and she picked it up on her way to my house. Ben and Helen brought the two casseroles, one a cheesy potato, the other a green bean. All I did was make scratch rolls, but the butter comes from Kroger, too, not my one cow who has passed away.

God bless her! I hope there's a Cow Heaven, because Arthur loved ol' Bessie like a child. Then I think maybe she's with Arthur.

The conversation is enlightening, since I'm hearing for the first time in a month what's going on in the world. I'm relieved North Korea hasn't yet bombed America, and people are still investing in the stock market. Actually, I don't find those subjects too interesting.

Around two o'clock, we all gather in the pasture where Arthur kept his cows. I have Arthur's urn in my hands and, somehow, I don't want to let go. Claire senses my hesitation. "Mama?"

I love the way my daughter says, "Mama." There's charm and endearment, compassion and love, in the word of mystical beauty.

"Yes, dear." I lock my robin-blue eyes on hers.

"Do you want me to commit Daddy's ashes to the universe?"

Well, that was a new way of thinking about throwing Arthur away. I suppose if he committed to the universe, I'm glad for him.

"No, I'll do it, Claire."

I open the urn and toss Arthur's ashes as high in the air as I can. A burst of wind carries them away as we watch as long as we can see one fleck of ash. "Goodbye, darling," I tell Arthur. "I'll be seeing you." And I turn to walk back to Ted's Mercedes Benz.

As we drive back to the house, I recall the song, "I'll be seeing you," and begin humming it. I will always remember today.

About the Author

M. Sue Alexander is the author of the 12-novel Christian series entitled *Resurrection Dawn 2014*, and a follow up series: *Time of Jacob's Trouble*. Her interest in the biblical prophecy came early in her teens due to prophetic dreams of what the End Times would look like.

This independent novel is different from any she's written since the voice is in First Person Present. It's a study on life and death.

M. Sue lives on a farm in Middle Tennessee with her husband and writes daily. Her love for writing will likely continue on as she walks out of this life into a glorious one God has prepared for believers.

View her website at: www.msuealexanderbooks.com
Updates on Linked-in and Facebook

www.ingramcontent.com/pod-product-compliance
Lightning Source LLC
Chambersburg PA
CBHW070549180626
46817CB00005B/1754